tuned in

EPISODE #5

school
spirit

by Julia DeVillers

introduction

This Journal Belongs to: ☆

☆ Maddy Elizabeth Sparks ☆

Private! Keep Out!!!

So here's the deal. I already tried out for cheerleading one time. For the football team. It didn't go so well. First of all, I didn't make it. Second of all, all my friends did. So I was all ... AUGH!!!

But football season is over. And there's one more season of cheerleading starting soon ... basketball cheerleading!

Basketball cheer tryouts are coming! And I've already started freaking out!

Because I'm trying out!

I'm going to get up there again! In front of the judges! In front of the other girls! And yell! And cheer! And clap! And flip! And trip!!

OK, but seriously. What if I trip? What if I fall? What if I yell out loud and my voice goes ...

BLARP! GLARK!!?

Way stressful. And not only that, but I found out just yesterday that ...

We have to try out doing two cheers. They gave us the words and the motions to one cheer. That's called the Team Cheer. I've practiced the Team Cheer.

The other is an Original Cheer. "Original" means we have to make up a cheer ourselves.

Yes! We have to write the words! We have to make up some moves! So I have to write MY own cheer! And make up MY own moves.

So here's my Original Cheer so far ...

Go Team! Win! Blarp! Glark!

(And then I trip and fall and totally humiliate myself)

OK. I am having problems making up my Original Cheer. I have no idea what I will do for my own cheer! I am so dooooooooooooooooooomed!

G2G ... gotta catch the bus.

I was on the bus home. I was sitting with Danielle. Haley and Brittany were sitting in the seat in front of us. They were hanging over, talking to us. Haley was looking at my autograph book.

The autograph book I brought with me to Toopalooza! I went to Toopalooza! It was this ginormous music fest! I mean, you should see who signed my autograph book!

Ashlee Simpson   Jessica Simpson   PLAY   Nikki Cleary

Jhene   Aaron Carter   Nick Cannon

"Just think, Aaron Carter's hand touched the pen that wrote this very word!" Danielle sighed, pointing.

"Careful," Haley said. "Don't smudge!"

"Blah blah," Brittany yawned. "Those autographs are old news. I have new news. Way more important."

Danielle kept flipping through the book.

"AHEM," Brittany cleared her throat real loud. "I said, I have NEWS."

"Look! That one says 'To Maddy!' How cool is that!" Haley pointed at the autograph.

Brittany cleared her throat again.

"Oh!" Haley jumped. She closed the book and sat up straight. "Sorry, Brittany, sorry! What's the news! Tell us the news!"

"No, forget it," Brittany said. "If you just want to look at Maddy's book for the kazillionth time ..."

"No really, tell us, please!" Haley begged.

Brittany waited.

"Please!" Danielle said.

"Oh, OK," Brittany said. "I'll tell you. The new news is that tryouts are going to be open this time. That means everyone can come watch! I heard my Mom talking about it on the phone last night."

Brittany's mom is the cheerleading coach. Brittany gets all this inside info. I don't think she's supposed to know all this stuff! Or tell us! But she does.

"Everyone who?" I asked.

"You know, like everybody," Brittany said. "Parents. Anybody from school who wants to stay and watch."

OK, about this news. This was **NOT** good news! I mean, last time I tried out it was bad enough. I embarrassed myself in front of the judges and the coaches!

But this time ... I'm going to embarrass myself in front of ... EVERYONE????

Now I am seriously **FREAKING OUT**.

"How cool will that be?" Brittany said.

"Way cool!" Haley agreed with her. And then she stopped. "Um, but why is that cool?"

"Because everybody will get to see my double back handspring, of course," Brittany said. "Flip, flip, and bam! I'll stick it!"

"You'll be soooo awesome, Brittany!" Haley said. Brittany smiled at Haley. Danielle and I weren't smiling.

"That kinda makes me nervous," Danielle said. "Trying out in front of everyone."

"Well," Brittany said. "When you're a cheerleader you have to be out in front of everyone, Danielle. Maybe you're nervous because of that little problem you have with your tuck jumps?"

Danielle shlumped down in her seat.

"I finished writing my Original Cheer," Brittany said. "You guys are going to be all WOW! when you hear it."

"How come we have to make up our own cheers this time?" I asked her.

"My Mom said the judges decided they want to get an idea of our personalities," Brittany said. "To judge our individuality and our creativity!"

"I can't think of an Original Cheer," Haley said. "Brittany, will you help me?"

"Well, I'm pretty busy," Brittany told her. "With my own cheer stuff."

"But you're done writing your cheer," Haley whined. "You had a head start since your mom told you about it last week."

"But I have to keep practicing my double back handspring," Brittany said. "It's way difficult. I have to stay focused. Sorry. Can't help you."

Haley's head disappeared as she sat back down in her seat.

"Yeah, right," Danielle whispered to me. "She's just scared of the competition."

"Huh?" I whispered back.

"Brittany won't help anyone else because she doesn't want anyone to get better than her," Danielle said. "Yeesh. But if you want to practice, call me."

"What are you two whispering about?" Brittany demanded. "Maddy, are you done with your Original Cheer? Is it ready? Is it any good?"

"We only found out about making up an Original Cheer yesterday," Danielle said. "Give her a break."

Yes! Give me a break! Because ...

ACK! Not only do I have to make up an Original Cheer. But people are going to watch me do it! Probably going, Poor Maddy. She didn't make it last time. And now I get to see why!

ACK! ACK, AND DOUBLE ACK!!! I'M FREAKING MYSELF OUT!

Quick, I need to take my mind off this. I opened up my autograph book.

"Maddy," Brittany said. "Don't you think we've had enough of you always talking about Toopalooza."

Huh?! I mean, I didn't even say one thing!! I was just looking at my autograph book!

"I mean, REALLY, Maddy," Brittany said. "Don't you think you've had enough good stuff happen to you lately? Being part of the TOO Crew? Going to the music fest?"

"Yeah," Haley said. "And now you're trying to make cheerleading. And even maybe taking Danielle's spot away from her."

Danielle shlumped again.

"Maybe you should think again about trying out for cheerleading," Brittany said. "Let something good happen to someone else for a change."

Oh.

Now it was my turn to shlump. Because maybe it was true. I did have a lot of good things happening lately. Maybe I should give someone else a chance. Maybe I should just ...

Take my name off the list for tryouts!

Get out an eraser! And ...

Un-sign up!

The bus pulled up to my street. It was my turn to get off.

"OK, bye," I said.

"Bye," Danielle and Haley said.

"Byeeeee, Maddy," Brittany was all like waving and smiling.

"Maddy always gets everything good happen to her," I heard Brittany say. "It's just not fair."

chapter 1

It started to rain on me when I walked home from the bus. I was seriously soggy by the time I got home. I walked in and called out, "Is anyone home?"

"I'm upstairs on the computer," Dad yelled down. "Be right there."

Wonder why Dad was home early.

"OK!" I yelled back.

I was still feeling cranky. Crabby. Confused about what Brittany said. I mean, Brittany was always kinda jealous that I got to do TOO Crew stuff. But I helped her so she could do stuff, too. I helped her sign up with a talent agency. And she got to help out at Limited Too once, too.

OK, so she didn't get to go to Toopalooza.

But then ... I didn't make cheerleading like Brittany did! This was all so confusing. I was tired just thinking about it.

I went into the living room and flopped on the couch. I pulled the big blanket over myself.

"Hey!" something was already under the blanket!

Zack! My brother, Zack! In his pajamas.

"Sorry," I said. "I didn't see you under there."

"Gibbe that back," he said. "I'b all freezing."

"What's up with you?" I asked him.

"I'b sick. I hab a cold,' Zack said. And then he sneezed. ACHOO!

And wiped his nose on his arm.

"Gross, Zack," I said. "Get a tissue!"

"Can you get me one?" he said. "I'm too weak to stand up and get them."

Then he sniffed.

Oh, all right. I got up and got him a box of tissues. At least I wouldn't have to watch him snot all over his arm. I tossed the tissues at him and sat back down.

PPPPPTTTTTTTARP!

A gross noise came from the cushion.

"ZACK!" I yelled, pulling out a whoopee cushion.

"Heh," he laughed weakly. Then he coughed.

I threw the whoopee cushion at him. He did look kinda pathetic. I sat down. No noises this time. Except Zack blowing his nose. Which sounded like Honk!

"What's on?" I asked him.

"Pet Channel. The Dogstacle Course Competition," Zack said. "These dogs do this obstacle course. Way cool!"

I watched the dogs lining up for their turn! Look at all the cute dogs! Pomeranians! Terriers! Saint Bernards! King Charles Spaniels!

Yes! I love dogs! I love them all!

Do I have a dog?

Nope! I don't. Dad says, not yet. Not ready. Just not.

But I think he's going to crack. Because lately when I ask him for a dog, he says ...

We'll see.

Yes, it's true! He says "We'll see!" That is so way better than ...

NO! And I think soon he might say ...

YES! That we can get a dog!

In the meantime ... I'm working on it.

Just then Dad walked in.

"Hi, Dad!" I said. "What are you doing home?"

"I stayed home with Zack today," he answered. "What are you watching?"

"Dogs! Very smart and talented dogs!" I told him.

We all watched the TV. The first dog was starting the obstacle course. It was a big German Shepherd.

"Nice looking dog," Dad commented.

"Yes!" I said. "It is!"

The German Shepherd jumped over a gate. Like it was nothing! Then it picked up a dog bone and ran through a tunnel ... and gave the bone to its owner. Go, dog, go!

"Look how that dog can fetch things. We could teach our dog to fetch you things, Dad," I said. "Like the newspaper!"

"Well, that would be a good trick," Dad agreed. The German Shepherd then ran through some hoops and completed the course in 32 seconds.

"Yay!" I clapped. "Good job!"

The next dog contestant was a dachshund with a little pink bow attached to her collar.

"Heh!" Zack pointed. "A little wiener dog's going to try it."

The wiener dog tried to jump over the gate. But she was too short. She knocked the gate down.

"Whoops," I said.

But the wiener dog didn't give up! She kept going! She ran to the dog bone and picked it up in her mouth. But the poor doggie kept dropping the bone. But then she picked it up! And then she dropped it again.

The wiener dog ran through the course. Slowly. Knocking things over. Not doing well.

"This dog is pathetic," Zack said.

"Well, not all dogs can do obstacle courses," I said. Poor doggie! "Go doggie!" I cheered for the little wiener. It finally finished. "At least it didn't give up. It should win a prize just for that."

A commercial came on.

"Dog owners!" the announcer announced. "Are you having a hard time training your dog?" And then a dog was on the screen chewing some shoes.

"Oh," Dad said. "I would be very unhappy if that happened to my shoes."

Then there was a dog scratching on the furniture! I saw Dad look at our new couch and make a face. Oh no!

"Zack! Turn the channel!" I hissed at him. Argh! He was ruining our chances!!!

Zack reached for the remote ... but not before ... Oh no!

The dog on TV was ... um ... going inside the house!

"Heh!" Zack laughed. "Check that out! That dog is pee –"

I grabbed the remote and changed the channel QUICK! And gave him a look.

"What?!! That was funny," Zack said. "That was a cool dog. I'd name that dog, Sprayer! Dog of Major Soakage!"

Argh!

"Yes, that's the problem with dogs," Dad said. "Chewing! Scratching! And the other problem! The whole spraying thing!"

He got up and walked away.

"Zack!" I said. "Did you hear Dad?!! We're never going to get a dog this way!"

ARGH!!

"Oh," Zack said. "I guess maybe I shouldn't have said that Sprayer stuff."

DUH!

I got up and went into the kitchen. Argh. I would never get a dog! Way frustrating!

Also another thing is way frustrating ...

I've got to write an Original Cheer. I got out a notebook and a pen. Ready? OK. (That's what you say before you say a cheer ... Ready? OK!) So.

Ready, OK?

> *"My name is Maddy!*
> *And I'm here to say!*
> *I'd be a good cheerleader!*
> *Hey, hey, hey!"*

Stupid.

"My name is Maddy!
And I'm here to say!
I'd be a good cheerleader
If Brittany would stay out of my way!"

I erased that one real quick. Take no chances anyone would see it.

"I'm Maddy!
I want to be on this team!
I can't think of a good cheer!
I'm going to scream!"

AUGH!!!! I was coming up with ...

NOTHING!

Maybe I should practice my moves instead. I went back into the family room. The only place with enough space.

I did a jump! A herkie! A clap, clap, twist!

"Hey," Zack said from the couch. "Get out of the way."

"Zack," I said. "I am so not in your way. I'm behind you. You can still see the TV."

"But you're going bump, thud, bang and all that," Zack said. "Like an elephant."

"I have to practice my cheers, Zack," I said. "This is the only place to do it."

Then the phone rang. I answered it. It was Brittany.

"Hi Maddy," she said. "Do you have the pages we're supposed to read for Wellness? I left my planner at my private cheer tutor practice. And guess what? My private cheer tutor said that my double back handspring was off the hook!"

"That's great. Hold on, let me get the homework," I mumbled. I told her the page numbers.

"Thanks," Brittany said. "So did you write your Original Cheer yet? Is it any good? Are you psyched about it?"

"Um, I have call waiting," I said. "Sorry. Gotta go!"

I hung up. OK, OK. Maybe I shouldn't have made up that excuse! But that girl makes me STRESSED! I went back to my cheer.

Jump! Herkie! Clap, clap!!

"Maddy!" Zack yelled. "You're hurting my ears!"

"Zack! This is the only place I can practice my jumps," I told him.

"Go outside," he said.

"It's raining outside," I said as I pointed to the window.

"And your point is?" Zack said.

"Zack!" I screamed. "Brittany has a private cheer tutor, OK? I have to practice these cheers and this is the only room big enough. If I don't practice, I'll totally embarrass myself!"

"Guys!" it was Dad. "What's the problem?"

"I have to practice my cheers," I said, all stressed. "And Zack won't let me."

"And I have to watch TV because I'm all sick," Zack said. "And Maddy won't let me."

Dad looked at me.

"Maddy, you do seem a little stressed. Maybe you should take a little break," Dad said.

Zack gave me a look like HA!

Just then the phone rang again. Dad got it.

"Maddy, it's Lauren," he said.

Lauren! From Limited Too headquarters! She was in charge of the TOO Crew! Me, Kacey, Isabel, and Claire. I grabbed the phone.

"Hi!" I said.

"Hi, Maddy," Lauren said. "I've got the next assignment for you girls. It involves helping out at headquarters. This assignment is a little less glamorous than some of your others. But it would really help us out. And help you get ready for your next assignment."

Great! Cool!

I would go to Limited Too headquarters ... tomorrow! With the TOO Crew!

```
From: MizIs
Send to: Maddyblue
CC: SpaceyKacey, ClaireBear
Subject: CU @ TOO 2morrow!!!

Hey Maddy! Don't U have cheer tryouts soon?!?!
We'll have TOO Crew School of Tryouts! Wear
clothes 2 cheer in!

TTYL, Isabel
```

chapter 2

I walked into Limited Too headquarters with my Mom. It's a really big white building with lots of glass windows.

I was psyched to be here. I didn't even feel nervous anymore! We got buzzed in. I went right up to the desk.

"Hi Maddy," both of the women behind the front desk said. They both knew my name! I felt kinda famous! I stuck my visitor's badge on my shirt. I was wearing a white t-shirt with blue flowers on it and blue track suit with my Reeboks.

"Hi Pam. Hi Maddy," Lauren said.

"Have fun, Maddy," Mom gave me a hug goodbye. "I'll pick you up in a few hours."

"The rest of the TOO Crew just got here," Lauren said. "We're going to head back to one of the conference rooms to start."

Lauren and I walked through a hallway.

I looked out the glass windows at the rain. I saw picnic tables and chairs.

"Sometimes we eat lunch out there," Lauren said. "When it's not raining, that is."

We walked into a big conference room. The TOO Crew was there!

Kacey! And Isabel! And Claire!

"Maddy!" they said. Kacey jumped up and showed me where to sit. Isabel smiled and gave me a wave. Claire gave me a hug.

And ... the door opened. And in walked ... Oh no ...

PIPER and SIERRA. Two girls who were ...

Rude! Nasty! Seriously snobby!

"Hiiiiiiii!" Piper walked in. "Sorry I'm late. I was auditioning for a part in a radio commercial. They LOVED me."

See what I mean?

"Yeah, and I went with her," Sierra said. "Piper was great. She had to say, 'Oh no! I've got a zit!'"

Piper gave her a look like, OK, that's enough. But Sierra didn't see it. She kept talking.

"And then she said, 'Oh gross! It's a big one right on my nose!'"

"ANYWAY," Piper interrupted loudly, sitting down. "That just shows how good an actor I am. Because I have perfectly clear skin but I could pull off those lines so believably."

"Well, now's a good time to give you directions for your next assignment," Lauren said. "I told you all that this is not very glamorous, but it's very helpful. We'd like you to help us put together goody bags for an event we are sponsoring."

I saw Piper roll her eyes.

"I'm here to be an office slave? Way boring," she whispered. Loud enough for us to hear, but not loud enough for Lauren to hear.

Kacey looked at me like Ugh! There she goes again.

"Psst, Maddy!" Isabel leaned across Kacey. "If we get a break, we'll start The TOO Crew School of Tryouts!"

OK! I needed it! I had been practicing. Every night! But I still felt like ... I wasn't getting any better.

When we were on our trip to Toopalooza, the TOO Crew had said they would help me!

Kacey would help me be peppier, 'cuz that girl is seriously smiley!

Isabel would help me with the jumps and tumbling. Because that girl could moooove!

Claire could help not be so klutzy. Because she is like this graceful dancing girl.

Lauren assigned us rooms as partners. My first partner was Isabel! We were in a meeting room called The Tree House.

"One of the prizes in the goody bags is candy," Lauren told me and Isabel. "So please open the packages of candy. Then put one candy from this pile and one candy from the other pile in each goody bag."

"No problem," Isabel told her.

"I'll be back in 20 minutes," Lauren said. "If you don't finish, don't worry. And if you finish faster, just hang out for a few."

Lauren left.

I looked at all the bags of candy. There were tons and tons of bags! TONS!

Where do we start?!

"Let's make a game plan," Isabel said. "Break it into baby steps. How about you open the packages, and put them in a pile. I'll put the candy in the bags. Then we'll switch."

OK!

We started.

"So, Maddy," Isabel said, stuffing bags. "We can talk about

cheerleading stuff while we do this. How's it going?"

"Oh, OK I guess," I said. "Besides me being a SuperKlutz who isn't getting any better and is going to totally humiliate myself."

"So what's your game plan?" Isabel asked me.

"Um, to keep practicing?" I said. "And write my Original Cheer?"

Isabel smiled. We kept working on the bags. Open! Sort! Stuff! And then ...

We were done!

"Hey," I interrupted. "We're done! Your plan worked great!" We'd finished in only 10 minutes!

"This gives us time to work on your cheerleading game plan," Isabel said. "Do you have a pen and paper?"

I went into my backpack. I poked through my:

- ☆ Planner (it's red and black)
- ☆ HITCLIPS player (the new round kind)
- ☆ Blue fuzzy journal
- ☆ Candy necklace
- ☆ Book that I'm almost done with (the main character is this girl who's way funny!)

I took out my journal. I had a new gel pen! Pink with a fuzzy princess crown on the end of it.

"Cool pen," Isabel said. "OK, first we have to write down your goal."

Maddy's Cheerleading Tryout Goal: To make cheerleading!

"OK, now what do you have to do to reach that goal?" Isabel asked.

"Ohmigosh," I groaned. "I have a gajillion things to do! I have these two different cheers, and the words and the moves and the ..."

"Wait!" Isabel said. "That's way overwhelming. Break it down into little steps." Isabel began writing.

Maddy's Cheerleading Tryout Game Plan

1. Learn the Team Cheer's words
2. Learn the Team Cheer's moves
3. Write Original Cheer
4. Practice
5. Practice in front of an audience
6. Go to tryouts and do my best!!!!

Isabel stopped writing.

"Ack," I said. "Steps 5 and 6 freak me out."

"That's why you have to take it step by step," Isabel said. "If you do the first steps one at a time, you'll be fine by step 6."

Yeah, right. Not likely.

"So let's work on #1, Learn the Team Cheer's words," Isabel said.

"I already did!" I told her.

Isabel handed me the pen. I crossed off #1 on the list.

"All right!" Isabel said. "You did it!!"

"Yeah," I said. "But that's just the first step! And that was the easy part. Now the hard part. Now I have to do steps 2 to 6!"

"Nope," Isabel said. "Now we celebrate. Each time you do one of the steps, you have to have some reward or something. You have to reward yourself for Step 1!"

"Girls!" Lauren stuck her head in the door. "How's it going?"

"Great," we told her. "We're done."

"Good job," Lauren said. "Let's take a break. Ice cream anyone?"

Yum!

"Perfect!" Isabel said. "That's the reward for doing Step 1!"

We followed Lauren down a hall.

"How do you know all this stuff?" I asked Isabel. "I mean, you sound like a teacher. Or like someone's mom or something."

"From my older sister Jessica," Isabel said. "She competes in all this stuff ... track, math competitions, play tryouts. She's always setting goals and making these plans. It's not just for cheerleading. You can use a game plan for anything."

We walked into the cafeteria and saw ...

Kacey! And Claire! Eating ice cream! They waved at us and we went into the ice cream line.

YUM!

Maddy's List of Fave Foods!

- ✓ Mac and cheese!
- ✓ Quesadillas!
- ✓ Pizza!
- ✓ Curly french fries!
- ✓ ICE CREAM!!!!!!!!!!!!!!!!!!!!!!!!!!!!!!!!!!

Piper and Sierra walked up behind us in line.

"Hello, Piper! Hello, Sierra," Isabel said. "How did your goody bag preparation go?"

They ignored us.

"Our goody bags were great," Isabel answered herself, pretending they had said something. "Thanks for asking."

I cracked up!

When people are rude to me I'm usually all like, Oh no! What did I do! They make me feel so stupid! But Isabel is cool about it. She mostly just ignores them! She's like, Those people are rude! But that's their problem.

Piper rolled her eyes.

"This is so lame-o," Piper said. "Stuffing goody bags? I mean, puh-lease. I am about to break into national celebrity stardom and what am I doing? Office work?"

"Yeah!" Sierra said. "This is so lame we're doing this."

"Well, see Sierra, these things are fine for you," Piper said to her. "But me? I am the Tako Tiko Princess ..."

Ugh! Blugh! That girl drives me cra-zay!!!

Isabel and I ordered our ice cream and brought it over to

where Kacey and Claire were sitting. Piper and Sierra were looking around for seats ... the cafeteria was pretty full.

Don't sit with us don't sit with us don't sit with ...

They came over. And sat with us.

Blugh.

"Maddy, are you getting excited to try out for cheerleading?" Kacey was asking.

I shrugged. More like nervous! And then Piper started in ...

"Maddy? Cheerleading? I mean, the girl who knocked over the catazine shoot? The girl who spilled whipped cream all over me at Toopalooza? That girl can't even walk straight."

"Everybody trips sometimes," Claire said.

"Maddy would be a great cheerleader!" Kacey said, all sticking up for me.

Piper shrugged. "That I'd like to see."

"Well, maybe you should," Kacey said. "Maybe Maddy will have to show you some of her serious cheerleading moves. Right, Maddy?"

Um ... uh ....

"Show us a cheer!" Sierra said.

What? No way!

"I'm not ready," I whispered to Isabel, all frantic. "Steps 2 to 6! Steps 2 to 6!"

"Maddy's got a few things to do first," Isabel told everyone. "Ask her next time. She'll be ready."

I will?

"Yes," Isabel said, looking at me. "You will."

chapter 3

Next up was me and Kacey working together! Our job was to unwrap CD's and put them in bags. We split them up into piles.

Kacey was like zooming through the pile! Super fast!

Unwrap! Stuff! Unwrap! Stuff!

"You are seriously speedy!" I told her. "We're going to finish this in 5 minutes!"

Kacey laughed. But I was right! She totally finished her pile! And then helped me with mine!

"OK," Kacey said. "It's my turn for The TOO Crew School of Tryouts!"

"I'm on Step 2," I showed her. "That's Isabel's plan for me. I know the moves. I just don't know if I'm good enough at them."

"OK, so you're supposed to work on your moves?" Kacey said. "OK! Show me your cheer!"

I got up. Feeling a little stupid. But getting used to this.

I did my cheer! I tried really hard with my arm movements! And my jumps! And my stamps and my claps!

"Hm," Kacey said. "Not bad but ... where's the smile? Like, aren't you cheery for your team?" Kacey asked. "You need some Smiley Lessons!"

Well, she's the best person to give smiley lessons. That girl is seriously smiley!

"OK, how 'bout this?" I said, smiling. And feeling kinda dumb. "I'm smiling."

"Too fake! Too forced!" Kacey laughed. "You can't just go up there and go, OK! Time to smile!"

"What do I do?" I asked her.

"Start smiling even before you go up there! Smile on your way up! Smile right at the judges!"

"When I'm nervous, it's hard to smile," I confessed.

"Think of something happy," Kacey suggested.

Think of something happy? Hmmm ...

- ★ Cute little puppies!
- ★ Vacations at the beach!
- ★ Swimming!

"Yay!" Kacey did a little happy dance. "It's working! You're getting smiley!"

I was!

"Now, think about happy things while you're cheering! Go, Maddy, go!"

And then I did my cheer again. This time I was smiley!

"Yay!" cheered Kacey. "And now ... Jump higher! Bounce more! Jump! Bounce! Pep! Spirit! Higher! Think of your happy, happiest things!"

I jumped! I bounced! I pepped!

I thought of happy things! My guinea pig, Sugar! Toopalooza! Being part of the TOO Crew!

"YAY!!!" Kacey said. "You looked super spirity! You were like Super Maddy Smiling girl!"

Kacey was clapping and all happy for me!

I was happy for me, too. And I was still all smiley!

Lauren stuck her head in the door.

"Wow, looks like you girls are in a good mood in here," Lauren said. "Positive attitudes. That's what I like to see!"

"We finished up," I told Lauren. "Kacey is super speedy."

"And Maddy is now super smiley!" Kacey said.

"Excellent," Lauren said. "Kacey, why don't you join Isabel in that room. And Maddy, how about you come with me to The Tree House?"

Now it was my turn to be partnered with Claire, right?

Wrong! I walked into the room and saw ...

Piper.

Yipes! Eek!

Me and Piper? Together? Alone in a room?

"Oh," Piper looked up. "It's you. Yeesh. We'll probably have to spend all our time fixing what you screw up."

I wanted to say, Hey! That's not true!

But I didn't. That girl makes me crazy. But she also makes me way nervous. Too nervous to say anything back. So I just sat down.

We started stuffing goody bags with lip gloss. La la la, stuffing, stuffing. Not saying anything. Doo doo doo. It was really quiet in there. Maybe I should say something. Anything.

"These are cool goody bags," I tried.

Piper nodded.

"So, um, how was your audition for that commercial?" I asked her.

"OK, look, I don't need you rubbing that in," Piper said. "How was I supposed to know the people who made the zit cream were there, OK? I mean, it really did smell bad. I was just being honest when I said that."

Oh. Well, maybe I shouldn't have said anything.

La, la, la, stuffing, stuffing ...

"So you're trying out for cheerleading?" Piper asked me.

I nodded.

"Isn't that Brittany girl captain of your cheerleaders?"

"Um, yes," I answered. Piper and Brittany had been friends. For like a day. They'd been on the same team at *TOO's U-Pick Challenge* contest. Then Brittany kinda screwed things up for their team.

So Piper liked Brittany about as much as she liked me.

Meaning, not much.

"In MY school, our cheerleaders have to have some talent and coordination," Piper said. "I mean, you guys must have some school. Brittany, the girl who wrecks things. And you, the girl who knocks over things."

My face turned bright red. I couldn't think of anything to say. That girl makes me so ...

— NERVOUS! —

But OK, we only had a couple more minutes. I would ignore her.

"You forgot to put one in that bag," Piper pointed. She gave me a look like DUH!

"Oh, yeah," I said. I did make a mistake.

"Hurry up, Snail," Piper said. "We'll never finish if you're so slow."

I tried to go faster. I mean, Piper kept giving me these looks. I couldn't concentrate. It was making me start to screw up!

Lauren stuck her head in.

"Girls, it's time to wrap it up," she said.

"Sure!" Piper said, all nice to Lauren. "Thank you, Lauren!"

We got up and followed Lauren out.

"That's the first time I didn't finish," Piper hissed. "Thanks to you, we didn't get all these bags stuffed. Snail Girl."

"Well, Lauren did say that some of these assignments would take longer so we wouldn't be able to finish" I whispered back.

Piper just snorted. Rolled her eyes. Like, yeah right. If I didn't have to be partnered with YOU!

"Look, you may have beat me in the *TOO's U-Pick Challenge*," Piper whispered. "But any other competition? I will CRUSH YOU!"

YIPES!!

chapter 4

We were all hanging out in the lobby, waiting for our parents to pick us up.

"I can't believe I had to be partnered with Piper," I groaned.

"That would be pretty bad," Kacey admitted.

"She was way mad at me," I said. "Said I screwed everything up."

"Did you really screw up?" Kacey asked.

"Well, we didn't finish," I told her. "But Lauren didn't seem to mind that we didn't get it done. There were a lot of bags. And Piper was making me all crazy in there. She kept giving me these looks. It kept messing me up!"

"That's so mean," Claire said.

But then Isabel goes, "You can't let that get to you."

"But you should've seen her looking at me! Seriously nasty looks!" I told her. "They made me all shaky! I couldn't concentrate!"

"Still, you shouldn't let her get to you," Isabel said.

Yeah, right! I mean, if someone's giving me dirty looks? That really freaks me out!

"Hey, that makes me think of something," Isabel said, "While we're sitting here, we should have The TOO Crew School of Tryouts!"

They told me to get up and do my cheer. OK, I felt a little dumb! But I also needed the HELP!!!! So I stood up.

Isabel whispered something to Kacey. They all sat in a row pretending they were judges.

I started my Team Cheer.

> *"Green and white!*
> *Let's fight ...!"*

I smiled at the judges like Kacey had told me. I jumped. I smiled at Claire! I smiled at Kacey! I smiled at ...

Isabel. Who was not smiling back. She was giving me a look, like puh-lease. You are so not doing well, here.

"What?" I stopped.

"Keep going," Isabel said. So I did. But she kept looking at me. Like I was wayyyy bad or something! I stopped in mid-jump. And went, thud!!!

"WHAT?!!" I said. "Why are you looking at me like that? Am I that BAD?"

"Aha!" Isabel said. "You're not supposed to stop. Keep going."

"Maddy, keep going!" Claire said. So, I did. I tried! But with Kacey and Isabel looking at me all weird, I just couldn't do it! I sat down.

"OK, forget it," I said. "I'm bad. Way bad. I give up."

"Why do you think that?" Isabel asked.

"'Cuz you guys keep looking at me like that!"

"We did that on purpose," Isabel explained. "You said you got all nervous when Piper gave you looks. You have to be ready for anything. What if it happens at cheerleading tryouts?"

"What?" I said. "Piper is going to be at my tryouts?"

"No, I mean what if someone gives you dirty looks? Like a judge or something?" Isabel answered me.

"Well, the judges are always the coaches! Grown-ups! They don't give dirty looks. They're just all serious!"

"Can't hurt to be prepared, just in case," Isabel shrugged.

"OK," I asked them. "What am I supposed to do?"

"Ignore them," Isabel said. "It's not your problem, it's theirs."

Easy for Isabel! She's always cool and calm. Nothing bothers her!

"Keep smiling no matter what!" Kacey said.

"You don't have to lose your good manners," Claire said. "Just because someone else does."

Claire is seriously polite! But it was good advice!

"And, think of people who DO make you happy," Isabel said.

"Remember what it's all about!" Kacey bounced all over the place! "School spirit! Team spirit! Go, Maddy, go!"

"And we've gotta go!" Isabel said. "Our rides are here. Maddy, remember your game plan!"

I pulled out my goal sheet. Next up ... Write the Original Cheer. Then practice it. Then do it in front of people. Then do it at tryouts.

YEEK!!!! TRYOUTS! ACKKKKKK!!!!!!

I thought of what Isabel said. One step at a time.

chapter 5

I was in school. 7th period wellness. Wellness is always good. Because it means it's not the other alternating class. Every other day I have choir. And I am so not a good singer.

Coach Crosby came in to start the class.

"Team!" he announced. "I have news for you. Listen up!"

We listened up.

"For those of you new here, School Spirit Day is when different schools in our city compete in fun and healthful events. Usually, the grade above you attends School Spirit Day."

"Yeah! And this year our school will beat the Red Team!" somebody yelled.

We were all like YEAH! Beat the Red Team!!!! Because the Red Team is the team of our rival school. They've won School Spirit Day three years in a row! They get to keep a trophy in their school!

Our school is the Green Team. And we want that trophy!

"But," Coach continued. "We've just been asked to have some students in your grade, compete, too. And they will be students in my sixth and seventh period wellness classes."

Which means ....

US!!!! We are going to get to go to School Spirit Day!!!!!

We were all like, YEAH!!!

"Now we don't have much time to practice," Coach said. "So start getting into shape. Push-ups! Chin-ups! Pull-ups! Ups, ups and more ups! The ball is in our court! Let's take it and run with it! Let's hit the goal zone and score, score, score! Win win win!"

Everyone was like jumping all over and saying YEAH! Brittany was doing some cheer moves in front of me. My friend named Petie turned and gave me a hand slap from the next row.

Coach Crosby would be a seriously good cheerleader. Everyone was all like YEAH!

That will be so exciting to go! I couldn't wait to watch everyone compete. I would be all Go Green Team! Cheer 'em on to victory!!!

"So does that mean no homework tonight?" Petie asked.

"Incorrect!" Coach Crosby said. "There will be a quiz on the chapter tomorrow. School Spirit is a mental challenge AND a physical challenge. We have to keep our brains healthy and ...

blah blah blah blah

I tuned him out. I'd heard enough. A quiz. Ugh!

But School Spirit Day! Fun!

As long as I didn't have to compete. It would be fun to watch!

"And everyone has to compete in at least one event," Coach said. "Everyone. No slackers on Coach Crosby's team of superstars. Right?"

Oh. Right?

Yipes!!

Petie passed me a note.

Hi MAddy! WhAt do you wANt to compete in? Check one:

☐ RelAy rAce
☐ RunNing rAce
☐ ObstAcle coUrse
☐ Other

I answered her.

☑ Other... NONE OF THE ABOVE!!!

Danielle called me after school.

"So I'm feeling a little pressure here!" I said. "First cheerleading tryouts. Then making up Original Cheers. Now I have to compete in School Spirit Day! This is all so WAY nervous!!!"

"Relax, Maddy," Danielle said. "I hear School Spirit Day is seriously fun. I wish I had Coach Crosby so I could go."

Brittany, Petie and I had Coach for 7th period. Derek Hogan and Ryan Moore had him for 6th.

Yes! Ryan Moore! At School Spirit Day! On my team!

Ryan Moore! #1 on my Ultimate Crush List!

Dark brown hair. Deep blue eyes ....

Maybe he would be my partner. In the three-legged race! Where we would have to run together and put our arms around each other for balance and ....

"Earth to Maddy," Danielle was saying.

"Oh, yeah! Sorry," I sighed. "Well I'm nervous about School Spirit Day. 'Cuz I have to compete in something."

"Maybe it will be something good! Like ice cream eating," Danielle suggested.

"Or maybe it will be like one of those TV shows and I'll have to eat bugs?" I told her. "Or see how long I can stay in ice water?"

"Maddy!" Danielle was laughing.

"Or worse!" I continued. "What if I have to be in the event where you have to make up your own Original Cheer? And perform it in public? 'Cuz right now that's my worst nightmare!!!"

I am serious. I can't write this stupid Original Cheer.

"You are seriously stressed out!" Danielle said. "Do you want to hear my Original Cheer? Maybe it'll give you some ideas."

"Thanks! But no," I said. "And not because Brittany said we all have to keep them top secret in case we steal each other's. But 'cuz I need to think of something myself."

"OK, good luck," said Danielle. We said bye and hung up.

I sat down at the kitchen table. I had to write this Original Cheer. But everything I wrote was way stupid. I'd look dumb saying them. What did the judges want me to say? I didn't know!!!!

"Maddy? Can you get me some juice?" Zack asked. He was lying on the couch.

I got up and got him some juice. And sat down to write.

"I'm out of tissues," Zack said. He sneezed. ACHOO!

Argh! I got up and brought him some tissues. And sat down to write.

"Chicken soup would be tasty," Zack said.

"Zack! Enough!" I said. "I have to write this stupid cheer. I can't concentrate with you interrupting me every two seconds."

"But I'm sick," Zack said. "And bored."

"Turn on the TV," I said.

"Makes me dizzy," Zack said.

"Play a video game," I told him.

"Makes me weak," Zack said.

Wow, he must really be sick. But sorry. I have things to do.

"Well, just lie there and leave me alone!" I said. "I have to write this cheer!!!! It's stressing me out!!!"

"But I'm sick," Zack sniffled. "And I'm all lonely."

Oh. ALL RIGHT! I wasn't having any luck with my cheer anyway. I went over to him. He did look kinda sad. He did look pretty pathetic. His nose was all red. His eyes were all watery.

"You do look pretty yucky," I told him.

"Thanks," Zack said. "So. What's this Original Cheer thing. I bet I can help write it. My teacher told me that the story I wrote about a giant squirrel with rabies was very original."

"Um," I said. "Thanks. But no thanks."

"No, seriously. Whatcha got?"

I read my paper.

> "My name is Maddy! I'm here to say!
> We're going to win today! Yay!"

Zack was quiet. "What else?"

> "My name is Maddy,
> I'm here. To cheer."

"Boring," Zack said. "The judges will be all SNORE. How about this ..."

> "Get me a tissue! Get me some juice, too!
> Or I'll sneeze gross green snot, all over you!"

"Oh, ugh, Zack," I said.

"What's your excuse? Go get me some juice!
Go Maddy, Go Maddy, Go!"

Zack was cracking himself up.

Then all of a sudden ....

COUGH! COUGH! GAK!!!

Zack was having this major coughing attack. He curled up in the blanket. He looked pretty sick. Really sad.

"I'm sick," he whined. "Do a puzzle with me."

"Sorry," I told him. "Do a puzzle without me."

"But you're good at puzzles," Zack said. "I need you. I'm sick. Play with me."

Oh. I was actually feeling sorry for him. "Look, I'm sorry. But you have to leave me alone. I have to write my cheer," I told him.

"What's more important? Cheerleading or your poor sick little brother?" he asked. His face was all sad.

"Zack," I said. "I've got to write this Original Cheer. It's stressing me out! OK? OK. So Sh!"

"Maddy! Phone!" my Mom was yelling.

Maybe it was someone calling to say, "Original Cheer has been cancelled due to lack of interest!"

Or maybe even "Cheerleading tryouts have been cancelled! Everyone can make the team!"

I got up and got the phone.

"Hey, it's me!" said Brittany.

Or maybe it's Brittany! Calling to stress me out even more!

"I told Coach Crosby I'd paint some banners for School Spirit Day," Brittany said. "Want to help?"

Um, I should help. Team spirit and all. But ... I'd been kinda avoiding Brittany. 'Cuz she used to be just funny and silly and crazy! But lately she's also been mean!

"My Mom said nobody can come over my house," Brittany said. "But I could bring the stuff over to your house."

WELL ...

She was sounding all nice ... and ...

I had to admit something! I missed the old Brittany. We had fun! We had crazy times! Like the time we dressed up in our Halloween costumes and ran around my street. But it wasn't even Halloween that day!!!

"Zack's kinda sick," I told her.

"Oh, I don't care," she said. "We'll just tell him to scram!"

Maybe if she came over we could hang. She would remember our good times! And then she would turn back into ...

The Nice Brittany again!!!

So I said, "Yes! Come over!"

chapter 6

Brittany came in. We went to my room! Far away from Zack!!!!

"Hey, cool. That's new," Brittany said, pointing to my door. I had a puffy doorbell shaped like a smiley face.

I'd had it for a month. But Brittany hadn't been over in a loooooong time.

"I got it so Zack can't just bust in my room anymore. He has to ring the doorbell!" I told her.

We set up the stuff to make signs.

"I picked out my outfit for School Spirit Day," Brittany said. "Want to coordinate?"

Oh! Sure! Brittany hadn't asked me to coordinate in awhile.

"We have to wear the green team shirt of course," Brittany said. "And we def have to find green baseball hats. We can wear our pants that zip into capris or shorts. Then, if it's cold or hot or warm? We're set no matter what!"

Kewl!

We started to draw our signs.

☆ GO GREEN!!! ★
☆ Green team rocks!
☆

Then my bedroom doorbell went ...

DLING!!!

"Who is it?" I yelled.

JIGGLE, JIGGLE, PUSH!

Zack! Trying to bust in my room!

"We're busy! Studying! Go away!" I called out.

"Mom made you popcorn," Zack said.

"Did you sneak hot chili sauce on it, like last time?" I asked him, suspiciously.

"No," he said.

"Jalapeno pepper sauce? Hot wasabi sauce?" I asked.

"No," Zack said. "Mom just put butter on it."

I heard a noise. Crunch! Crunch!

"And lots of salt," Zack added.

I unlocked the door.

Zack came in carrying the bowl of popcorn. And chewing. Crunch! Crunch!

"Why are you in your pajamas?" Brittany asked him.

"I'm sick!" Zack said proudly. "I went through ten boxes of tissues already!"

He came over to Brittany, holding out the popcorn.

"Zack! Don't get your germs on me," Brittany said. Jumping back like get away!

And then, Zack sneezed. And not some regular little achoo.

AHHHH ... AHHHHHHH ... CHOOO!!!

All over the bowl of popcorn!

"Ewwwwww!" Brittany and I screamed!

"Man, there are boogers all over this," Zack said, looking at the bowl. "Extra salt and green slimy booger sauce."

"I think I'm going to puke," Brittany wailed.

"Gross! Zack, get out!!" I yelled at him. He sneezed his way out the door.

I turned to Brittany. "That was seriously sick. We can make some new popcorn."

"OK," Brittany said.

"Oh, this is so cute." Brittany looked closely at an orange and yellow picture frame sitting on my desk. "Did you make that?"

"Yeah," I said. I'd put a photo of me and the TOO Crew in it from Toopalooza.

"Oh, from Toopalooza," she said. I waited for her to be saying I was a show-off. But ... she didn't. She just goes, "Hey, is that all new stuff?"

Yup. I'd gotten some new:

> ☆ Lip glosses (Vanilla with sparkle! Blueberry swirl!)
> ☆ Nail polishes (Purple! Pale green!)
> ☆ Body glitter (Peach smell! Mint smell!)

"Let's put some on!" Brittany said.

We painted! Polished! And posed!

"Ooooh, you look fabulous," Brittany said. "So pop star. With a disco edge."

"And you look way glam," I told her. "Major movie star."

"Want to try on your clothes?" Brittany asked. She ran to my closet. "Oh, this pink top you wore last week? So cute on you."

"Thanks!" I said. Brittany was being so ... nice! So ... old Brittany!

"I'm going to wear this!" Brittany pulled out a long black velvet dress. "You wear the red one!"

Brittany put on a black hat. I put bracelets up my arms and all of my rings on my fingers. She put on a bunch of my chokers. Brittany put my hair up so it was all piled on top of my head.

"So supermodel," I said!

"Over the top," she agreed. "Oh, what's this?" She pointed at the rest of the stuff in my makeup case.

"That's just old dress-up makeup," I said. Kinda embarrassing! "Halloween stuff. You know, from when we were little kids and all."

Brittany pulled out a black makeup pencil.

"Come here," she said. Then she drew big black freckles on my face! And put bright orange lipstick on me!

"My turn!" I said. I colored her lips ... green!

We looked in the mirror and were totally laughing.

Then I turned on my radio and cranked it up.

I did my best supermodel walk. Brittany stood on my bed and blew kisses at the mirror. We were cracking up!

"Time for a modeling session, Brittany!" I said. I grabbed my sticker camera. "Strike a pose!"

"Did you say the word ... POSE?!" Brittany asked.

Huh? OH! Pose was the name of the group Brittany voted for in the *Too's U-Pick Challenge*. Those singers were rude! They were fake! And they lost! Partly because of, well, Brittany.

Oh no!!! I'd reminded her of her screw-up!!! I looked at Brittany to see how mad she was. But instead she was ...

Smiling!

"Ohmigosh," she said. "Ack! Don't say the word Pose!!!"

Brittany was laughing about it! She wasn't mad! Then she picked up my beanie frog. And threw it at me.

I threw it back! She picked up a beanie teddy and whomp! Then I whomped her on the head with a beanie kitten. Then ...

Stuffed animals were flying everywhere! Monkeys! Alligators! Puppies!

Even my ginormous hippopotamus ... WHOMP!! On my head!

We were jumping on the bed throwing stuffed animals! Ack! Eek! Brittany and I were ...

CRACKING up!

Then

RING!

We heard my front doorbell.

"Let's answer it!" Brittany said.

"But we're wearing ..." I looked at our crazy outfits.

"Dare ya!" Brittany said.

We raced down the stairs! I hope it's nobody we know! I hope it's the delivery person or just one of Zack's silly friends or ....

Brittany pulled open the door.

It was ... Brandon Nash and Derek Hogan!!!!!!! Two guys from our class.

"Uh, hi?" Derek said. "We're selling big cans of popcorn for a fund-raiser the basketball team –"

"But, uh, maybe it's not a good time," Brandon interrupted, looking at our outfits.

Ohmigosh. This was way embarrassing.

"Hello, Brandon and Derek," Brittany said, very serious. "We'd like to buy some popcorn. Do you have any sneeze flavored popcorn?"

"You mean cheese flavored?" Derek asked.

"No, sneeze flavored," Brittany said. "It's green? Maddy's brother makes it."

Ohmigosh. Ohmigosh. Brittany and I just went totally hysterical.

I was laughing so hard I had to lie on the floor.

"Uh, we'll stop back later," Brandon said, looking at us. And then Derek and Brandon ran down the steps and across the lawn.

I couldn't stop laughing! Brittany and I were lying on the floor like Ohmigosh! So funny!

"Can't breathe!" Brittany said, gasping. "Too! Much!

Laughing!"

I looked at Brittany and started laughing again!!!!!!!!

How cool was this???

"Maddy!" My mom called from upstairs. "Brittany's mom just called. She needs to head home, now."

We went upstairs to change back to regular. But we still couldn't stop laughing.

It was way fun.

chapter 7

This Journal Belongs to:

Maddy Elizabeth Sparks

Hello from Science class! I finished my worksheet. So I'm like, la la la. Time to write in my journal!

Look, some sparklies are sticking here.

It must be a little of the body glitter Brittany and I had put on last night! When we were having so much fun together. Me and Brittany! Laughing! Fun! It was great! I really missed the old Brittany. Because she got all nasty to me and everything. But she's back!

Today's going to be a good day. I can tell. Next up, Lunch period. And today I'm ready to talk to Ryan

Moore. Yes, I have my question ready:

"So, are you going to be at School Spirit Day?"

That's what I am going to ask Ryan. I have to practice what I'm going to say beforehand. He sits at my lunch table. And sometimes, I actually can talk to him. Not always! But sometimes I can do it without being all ... GAH!

9-29

Danielle and I walked out of class together. I saw Jordan Cooper.

"Hey Jordan!" I called out. "Are you going to lunch?"

Jordan came over and started walking with us. Then I saw Brittany in the hallway.

"Hiiiiii!" I said to Brittany. I was so happy to see her!

"Hi Maddy, hi Dani. Um, hi Jordan," Brittany said. Brittany didn't like Jordan much. But she said hi to her! Yes, this was the New Improved Brittany!

"Hey, do you want to get together and practice for tryouts?" Danielle asked us.

"OK!" Jordan said.

"Sure," I said. "Maybe we can all get together and help each other out after school tomorrow. Want to, Brittany?"

"Maddy, come here a second," Brittany said. She pulled me aside. "Are you sure you really want to do that?"

"Do what?"

"Practice with Danielle and Jordan Cooper? I mean, I heard Jordan is having trouble with her round-offs. Your round-offs are kinda good."

Huh?

"Um, so?" I asked her.

"She might ask you for help! And then you'd have to help her! And then she might be better than you and beat you for a spot! And Danielle? Face it, Jordan and Danielle are your COMPETITION!" Brittany said.

Yeah. That's true. Some people like Brittany were sooooo good at cheerleading. I mean, Brittany has been taking cheerleading since she was six! And her mom is the coach! And Haley wins gymnastics meets because she can flip, fly and tumble. So you know there are girls who are totally practically guaranteed to be on the team.

Then there are the leftover spots. For more regular people. Like me, Danielle and Jordan. But even if we are all competing, we could still help each other. I mean, friends are friends, right?

"I'm just saying," Brittany continued. "Just watch your back, OK?"

And she walked off.

"Let me guess," Danielle said. "Brittany will not be joining our cheerleading help session today."

We walked into the cafeteria and bought hot lunch. I sat down next to Jordan and Petie. Then Derek Hogan and Ryan Moore came and sat at the table with us.

That was the BEST part of third period lunch. Ryan Moore at my table!!!!

Right away Derek started talking.

"Yesterday me and Brandon went over Maddy's house to sell some popcorn. Brittany and Maddy were all wearing these crazy outfits and –"

ACK!!! He was telling everybody! Everybody including RYAN MOORE!

"All right!" I interrupted him. "We were having fun. That's all. No details!"

"But it's way funny!" Derek said. "So anyway, Brittany had green lipstick –"

"Derek!" I interrupted him. "Enough! Or I'll tell about the time you were in fourth grade and you were outside in your pj's and –"

I gave him a look! Derek was my neighbor so I knew what I was talking about!

"OK! I'm done with my Maddy and Brittany story!" Derek said. He took a bite of his cheeseburger.

We all sat there eating.

"I don't think that girl likes me too much," Jordan said.

"Who?" Petie asked her.

"Brittany," Jordan said. "She's always looking at me like she doesn't like me."

I didn't say anything. What's to say? It was true.

"Well, lately Brittany's been kinda ... um ..." I didn't know what to say. "But now she's better! She's back to her old self! We had soooo much fun the other night!"

"Hey. Here she is now," Ryan pointed out.

Brittany was heading over to our table. Huh. She's not in our lunch period. She has lunch fifth period with all the football cheerleaders so they could practice.

"Hi!!!!" I waved Brittany over to us.

Uh. Oh.

She didn't look too happy.

Brittany came over to my table.

"Maddy, I can't believe you did this to me," she said.

HUH?

"You invite me over and I catch stupid germs at your house," she said. "I just got back from the nurse's office. I'm sick, OK? They're sending me home."

Zack!

"Oh!" I said. "I'm sorry! I –"

"How could you do this to me, now?" she said. "What about School Spirit Day! And cheerleading tryouts are only days away!! I better not be sick for cheerleading tryouts," she said. She looked me in the eye. "Or there will be big, serious trouble."

Then Brittany was like HMPH! And she walked away.

"Whoa," Ryan said. "She is ticked."

"It's not your fault. You didn't get her sick on purpose," Petie said.

"Or did you?" Derek asked. "Did you get her sick on purpose so you could steal her spot on the cheerleading team?"

"What?! Of course not! No, don't even say it!" Yikes! Brittany might even believe that!

I felt Miserable! Awful! Terrible!

Brittany was sick!

And she was blaming me!

I thought about the Fun Brittany. The one who liked me. Was she gone ...

... forever???

chapter 8

I am at ...

SCHOOL SPIRIT DAY!

"Welcome to the Sixth Annual School Spirit Day where teams from six schools compete for the big trophy. Teams, are you ready?"

"YEAH!!!" we all yelled.

So we're at this big open field. There were all these games and sports and stuff everywhere. There were kajillions of people from other schools all over the place. It was way exciting! Five different teams all trying to win the trophy!

★ Red (BOO! Our rivals. And they always win. Ugh.)
★ Blue
★ Orange
★ Purple
★ Green! (That's us! Woo hoo!!!)

"Green Team, huddle!" Coach Crosby called out. We all went into a huddle. "Are you ready, team? This is the day we defeat! We destroy! We conquer! Are you with me!"

"YEAH!" we all yelled.

Coach handed out a list. He said every team would have two captains, a guy and a girl. Ours were Ryan Moore and Brittany. Ryan probably 'cuz he's a really good athlete. Brittany probably 'cuz she's a really good athlete. Or 'cuz she's bossy.

We each had to do one or two competitions.

"Too bad I can't do more than two," Derek said. "Because I would rock all of them!"

I checked my list. I would be doing Putt-Putt golf.

OK! That wasn't too bad! I can Putt-Putt!

I also noticed Ryan Moore would be doing the baseball throw contest and the grand finale ... the obstacle course! Brittany also was doing the grand finale obstacle course with him, since she was co-captain.

"Oooh, Ryan," Brittany squealed. "We're partners for the obstacle course!" She smiled. She giggled. At Ryan.

Oh! Um! I'm not liking that too much. I turned away.

"What are you doing?" I asked Petie.

"The rock climbing competition!" Petie said. "And the potato sack race."

We checked out the schedule. First up was the rock climbing competition!

"That's me!" Petie said.

"I'll go cheer you on! Go, Petie go!" I said. I did a little jump and clap! Yay Petie!

We headed over to the Rock Climbing Competition.

"Our first event is the rock climbing competition. Our first competitor is from the Green Team, Petie. She will be competing against the Orange Team's competitor, Kacey!"

"Go, Petie!" I was screaming when I heard the announcement. Did he say Kacey? I looked over at the rock climbing wall. Black hair in pigtails ... a big huge smile ...

YES!!! IT WAS KACEY! MY VERY OWN TOO CREW KACEY!

"Kacey!" I screamed. "It's me! Hi!!!!"

Kacey looked around. All of a sudden she started smiling and waving at me all crazy. How cool was that?! Kacey's school was here! She was on the Orange Team!

Kacey versus Petie! This was way exciting. Who would win?! My friend, Petie? My friend, Kacey?

The whistle blew.

"Go Petie!" I screamed with my team. We were all jumping and clapping all over the place. "Go, Green!" Then I screamed, "And go Kacey!"

"Did you just say, 'Go Kacey?'" I heard a voice beside me. It was Brittany. "Are you seriously rooting for the other team, Maddy?"

"Look, that's Kacey from the TOO Crew!" I pointed out.

"Excuse me, but rooting for the other team? Yeesh." Brittany said. "Total traitor."

Oh. True. I guess.

"Go GREEN!" I yelled. Way loud!

They were scaling the wall. Petie was climbing like a monkey! Kacey was bouncing up that wall like a super bouncer! Petie was winning! No wait, now Kacey! No Petie! No, Kacey! It was neck and neck!

"Go Petie!!! Go Kacey!!!" I was totally shrieking. Hey. They're both my friends, right? I'd sneak in a Go Kacey, too. "Go Green! GREEN is number one!!!"

They climbed and then ... Kacey reached the top.

And the winner was ... Kacey from the Orange Team!

I was so happy for her! First though, I ran over to Petie. I gave her a hug.

"Man, that girl was like SpiderGirl!" Petie said. "Wowza!"

"I'm sorry you lost! But that's my friend Kacey," I told her. "I'm going to go say congrats."

"Tell her I say congrats, too," Petie said. "She was awesome!"

I ran over to find Kacey. She was holding a ribbon for winning. Her teammates were like, Kacey rocks! Yeah!!!

"Maddy!" she screamed and ran over to me.

"You were so great!" I told her. "That was my friend Petie up there. She said to tell you that you were awesome!"

"Thanks," Kacey said. "Your friend was tough!"

Kacey was Super-Orange girl, wearing her orange shirt with orange track pants and sneakers with orange shoelaces in them. She even had an orange headband with soccer balls over it.

"I can't believe you're here!" I told her. "I never thought about it! Seeing someone from the TOO Crew at School Spirit Day!"

"How about two someone's," a voice behind me said.

ISABEL!!!

"ISABEL!" Kacey and I screamed.

Isabel was here, too! She was wearing a Purple Team shirt!!!!!
Isabel was on the Purple Team!

We were all jumping up and down! Hugging and like yay!!!!

"Kacey just won at rock climbing," I told Isabel. "She rocked!"

Get it, rocked? Rock climbing?! Ha, ha? Anyway.

"But I beat out Maddy's team," Kacey add. "Sorry, Maddy."

"Well, I'm psyched for you" I said. "But don't be too happy. We'll
crush you next time."

"Looks like the next event is starting," Isabel said. "Let's go
check out the Potato Sack Race!"

I saw Petie standing in her potato sack. There was someone
from each team standing in their sacks, too!

They all lined up at the start. Then the whistle blew! Everyone
started jumping and hopping toward the finish line! Go, Petie,
go!

Isabel, Kacey and I were all cheering for our teams! Go Green Team! GO Orange Team! Go Purple Team!

We stood on the side and cheered. "Go Petie, go!" I screamed. "You can do it! G-R-E-E-N!"

And Petie was winning! She was hopping and jumping and potato sacking her way right past us! A boy from the Red Team was right behind her! He passed us. Then a girl from the Blue Team hopped past us ...

Well ...

Almost past us ... because she tripped. She got tangled up in her bag! And wobbled toward us!

"Look out!" I yelled! "We're about to be potato sacked!"

We all jumped back. The Blue Team girl fell over right at our feet on the ground!

"Sorry! Excuse me! Oh, sorry!" she was saying. The girl took off her hat. She looked up at us and ...

CLAIRE??!!!

"Excuse me," she said politely. "I seem to be a little dizzy. So dizzy that you look like friends of mine."

It was CLAIRE!!!

"CLAIRE!" We all screamed.

"It's us! It's really us!" I said, all excited. "We're here at School Spirit Day, too!"

"Oh! My gosh!" Claire said. "It is you! I thought maybe I'd confused my brain when I fell."

The announcer was announcing the results. Petie from the Green Team had won!!!!

"Sorry, Claire. But I have to cheer for Petie a sec. Yay, Petie!!!" I screamed and clapped. "Go Green Team!!!!"

"I guess I lost that one," Claire said, stepping out of the potato sack. We all gave her a hug.

"This is so crazy we are all here!" Kacey said. "The TOO Crew has School Spirit!" She did a little cheer jump. And a round-off back handspring!

"Wow!" I said. "That was good!"

Kacey used to be captain of her cheerleading squad. She didn't do cheerleading this year at her school. She wanted to do soccer, instead. But she was still super-spirity!

"There's time for a break," Isabel said, looking at the schedule. "I've got my first event next. I'm doing a basketball throw."

"Let's get something to drink!" Kacey said. She pointed to an area with a big sign:

SPONSOR AREA

We headed over there. We got some bottled water from one table.

"Look!" Isabel pointed to the tables. "See anything familiar?"

I looked. There were piles and piles of bags. Bajillions of them! I recognized those bags! We had stuffed those bags! They were the Limited Too goody bags!

"Oh! Limited Too goody bags!" Claire said, clapping her hands. "That's what they were for! For School Spirit Day!"

And standing next to the table was Lauren! We all ran over to her.

"Well, look at this!" Lauren said. "A TOO Crew Reunion! I always knew I chose a spirited TOO Crew!"

Two girls from the Red Team were walking by. One of them pointed at the Limited Too bags. "Cool! I wonder what's in them!"

"WE know what's in those bags," I said. "We're the stuffers!"

"And thank you for your help putting them together," Lauren said. "Limited Too is one of the sponsors of School Spirit Day. Every girl will get a goody bag at the end of the event. The boys will get bags from that table over there."

"Kacey rocked the rock climbing!" I told Lauren. "But Claire got sacked in the potato sack race."

"I'm up next in the Basketball Shoot," Isabel said.

"Then I have to do Putt Putt golf," I said. I like Putt Putt! But I was getting a little nervous.

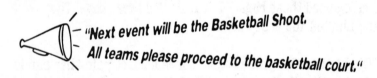
"Next event will be the Basketball Shoot. All teams please proceed to the basketball court."

"I'm up!" Isabel said, cheerfully. Lauren waved goodbye to us.

"Good luck, Isabel," I told her. "And Go Green!"

"Go Orange!" Kacey cheered.

"Go Purple!" Isabel said. "And Go me! Because I have to go to my event.

chapter 9

"Hey, Maddy!" Petie called out, waving. I went over and joined the rest of the Green Team to watch the Basketball Shoot.

Derek was playing for our team. We watched as the Orange Team went up. Then Blue! Then Red! Then it was time for ...

Green! Our team was up! Derek went up to the line.

"Go, Derek! You can do it!!!" I yelled. "Green team, green team! Goooo Green!"

Swish! YES! Two points for the Green Team! He ran over and high-fived all of us.

Last up, the Purple Team. That was ...

ISABEL!

"Cool," Derek said. "A girl. That means ... no competition for me."

I groaned.

Isabel also heard him. She smiled. She bounced the ball a few times.

"Go Isabel!" I yelled!

She shot and ... swwwwwwish!

Two points for Isabel!

"Yay, Isabel!" I screamed! "Nice shot"

And then I heard my name.

"Maddy!" It was Coach Crosby!

"Traitor," Brittany whispered. "You're busted."

I went over to Coach Crosby.

"Are you rooting for the other team?" he said.

Whoops!

"Um, that's my friend," I said. "I'm also way cheering for our team! Go Green!"

"Back in line, Sparks" he said. I ran back over to my place in line.

"You in trouble?" Petie whispered.

I don't know! Coach didn't seem mad. But maybe! I would cheer really extra loud for Green!

Derek was up. He dribbled. He shot! He scored! He did a little dance!

"Way to score! Show us some more!" I yelled. Really loud! So Coach would hear me!

Derek shot again! Three points! Whoo hoo!

"Three point shot!" I yelled. "You're really hot!"

"Who are you, Super Cheerleady Girl?" Brittany said to me.

Just then Coach walked by.

"Nice spirit, Sparks," he said.

Brittany looked at me. She was like, oh no! I'm being out-cheerleadered!

"Go Green! You are the best! I've ever seen!" Brittany started yelling. She ran by where Coach was standing. She ran out and did an aerial.

She was flipping! And flying! And was all Rah! Green Team! Rah!

Making sure Coach saw her.

Whatever! I turned back to the Basketball Shoot.

Isabel's turn!

"Go Isabel!" I called out. I couldn't help it! I was excited for her!!!!

Isabel went up to the basket. She shot ... Two points! Then ... a three point shot!

"Hey," Ryan Moore said. "That girl can shoot."

"That girl? She's got nothing on me," Derek said. "Green Team has nooo worries!"

The other teams were shooting! Scoring! And missing!

Derek was up again!

"Nothin' but net," he said. "This game is mine!"

"D-E-R-E-K! Derek all the way!" I cheered him on.

Coach Crosby gave me the thumbs up.

Isabel was up!"Yay, Isabel!" I screamed. Isabel waited a minute. She looked at the hoop. Swwwish! Two points! Swwwish! Three points!

"The top scorers are the Green Team and the Purple Team. *They are tied. They will now compete for first place."*

It would be Derek against Isabel! Ohmigosh! I could see Claire on the side with the Blue Team! I could see Kacey on the side with the Orange Team! We were all cheering!!

Derek got up to shoot. He scored! Two points for the Green Team!

I was jumping up and down! I was screaming, "Go Derek!"

We all high-fived him on the way back.

"Oh yeah!" Derek said. "Purple girl is history!"

So Isabel went up. She scored two points! Yeeees!

Then Derek! Three points! Then two!

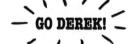
GO DEREK!

Ohmigosh! The pressure!

But Isabel stayed cool. She went up there and bam! Three points! Then two!

"I can't take this anymore!" I said. "This is way pressure!"

Derek got up there and shot and ... he missed! The crowd went Ohhhhhhhhhhhh!

"AUGH!" Derek yelled. He was way frustrated.

So Isabel had a chance. She bounced the ball a few times. She got ready. She shot and ...

SHE MADE IT!

"And the winner is the Purple Team! Isabel from the Purple Team is #1."

"AUGH!" Derek yelled. "I lost to a girl!!"

He stomped away. I ran over to Isabel.

"You ROCKED!" I told her. "Wow!"

"Thanks," she said.

Kacey and Claire ran over, too.

"Isabel, congratulations," Claire said. "And sorry your team lost, Maddy,"

"Yeah, I want Green Team to win! But I'm also psyched for Isabel!" I said. "But I better get back to my team!"

I walked back to where my team was standing. On the way, I checked the scoreboard.

Hey, Green Team won the egg-on-a-spoon relay, the frisbee toss, and the 50-yard dash! Green Team was in second place! Woo hoo!

SWEEEET!

Then I noticed Kacey came in second at the softball throw for her team! And Isabel had won the long jump! And Claire had come in second at the pop-a-balloon relay. Cool!

I moved out of the way for a girl in a Red Team shirt. She was trying to look at the scores, too.

"Red Team is winning. Of COURSE," the girl said all loud.

Wait! That voice! It was familiar. Oh no ... It couldn't be true. It was ...

PIPER!

chapter 10

PIPER was here???

That girl kept showing up EVERYWHERE!!!

And that was SO not a good thing.

OK, but I still had a chance. A chance to sneak off without her seeing me. I needed to disguise myself. I pulled my baseball hat low over my face.

Too low. Because yeah, Piper couldn't see my face. But I also couldn't see where I was going. I didn't see the bench! Bam! I walked right into the bench!

Ow! OW! OW!!!

I was hopping around! I couldn't help it! I mean, OW! My shin!

Red-face Rating: ★ out of ★★★★ stars.
Fortunately nobody saw me do that! Or did they???

Oh no! Piper looked up!

"Nice going," she said. Rolling her eyes. "Figures. Every time I hear a crash, I think it must be whats-her-face. The Clumsy Girl."

I wanted to say something. But OWWWW!

"I'm surprised your Green Team is doing as well as you are," Piper continued. "Considering you're on it. Didn't you trip and fall and ruin any events yet?"

Um, Uh ...

I tried to think of a good comeback! Think, Maddy! Think!

But ... ow?

It's hard to think when you're all in pain!

"Well, I must go join my team. I'm co-captain. Which explains why we're number one. Ta ta."

Piper smiled all ha ha. And walked away.

UGH! 🙁

That was so not right. I rubbed my shin. I limped back to my team.

"Hurry up, Maddy!" Brittany waved me over. "Chop chop! You're up next. You have to do the Putt Putt Course.

OK! It's my event!

I would stop thinking Piper. And start thinking Putt Putt.

I went over to the mini-golf course area. I'd be playing against one person on each of the other teams. OK. I could do this. Right?

I heard my name. Brittany was talking about me to someone.

"Maddy actually might be good for this one because we did Putt Putt at one of my birthday parties. And Maddy won!"

Yes! In third grade! That was a fun party. And I won a prize at Putt Putt! I smiled, thinking about it.

"We are ready to begin the Putt Putt Course!"

I got to go next to last. 'Cuz our team was in second place, we had the second best position. The Red Team would go last 'cuz they were in first place.

First, we had to hit the ball through the windmill. But if you hit it when the windmill was turning your ball would get bounced back!

A boy from the Blue Team went up and hit the ball. Oops! It hit the windmill and got knocked back.

Bummer!

The Orange Team girl's ball bounced back too!

Purple Team ... nope! Bounced back.

OK, it's my turn! I'm up!

I took the putter. I walked up.

I looked up. I could see Claire! She was smiling at me like, come on, Maddy! I smiled back.

I took a deep breath. The windmill's wheels were turning ... turning ... I tried to time it just right.

I hit the ball ... going ... going ... going ... GONE!

IT WENT THROUGH! It went through the windmill! Yay!

I looked up and I could see Kacey on the side bouncing all over! She was excited for me!

"Whew!" I heard Brittany say. "Major relief!"

Then a guy from the Red Team went up. He hit it and ... Zoom. Right through!

Round 2. Blue Team? Ball went through the windmill. Orange team? Ball went through the windmill. Purple Team? Nope, bounced back AGAIN!

"Ha ha!" said Brittany.

OK, I was up. I had to hit my ball up a hill and toward the hole. So ... OK ... OK! I hit it and ...

Up ... up ... over ... keep going! YES!!!! YESS!!!! The ball rolled right next to the hole! YEAH!!!

Everyone was cheering for me! Go Green! Yay!!!!!

Then the Red Team Guy was up. He hit and ... up ... up ... it went over the hill ... and rolled ... past the hole!

I was winning! Me! Go, Green!!!

Round 3. The final one. The other teams went up. They got closer to the hole. Except poor Purple Team Guy! He couldn't get it through the windmill at all!

"He stinks!" I heard Brittany say. I felt bad for him. Usually it was ME. Screwing up. In last place. Getting that look from Brittany. Instead I was getting ...

"Maddy! YAY Maddy! You're in first place!"

Yes, that was Brittany cheering for me!!! Then she says, "Win this thing! So I can go into the obstacle course as the winner!"

Or really ... she's cheering for herself.

Anyway.

I went up to putt. All I had to do was sink the putt. It was like 2 inches! I could do it! Right? I could do this?

"Watch," I heard from the crowd. "She'll trip and fall or something. She always does."

I knew that voice. Piper!

I tried to ignore her. But I looked up and saw her. Her face was staring at me. Like, miss! Miss! Miss the shot! Her eyes got squintier.

I started to shake! I can't help it! That girl makes me all nervous!

I just wanted ...

OUTTA THERE!

I hit the ball ... rolling ... oh no ... too hard!! It rolled past the hole. Buh-bye hole.

The whole crowd went ...

Ooooooooooh Nooooooooooo! My whole team groaned.

I lost!

I BLEW IT!!!!!!!!

"Good job, Maddy," Brittany said. "NOT."

I saw Piper laughing.

AUGH! AUGH! This was the worst! Why do I ALWAYS have to screw things up. I am the WORST School Spirit Day person ever!!!!

Don't cry don't cry don't cry don't cry!

I am a total LOSER.

The Red Team Guy went up there. And of course, just tapped his right into the hole. Tap! He won! Rah rah.

I looked at Piper. She gave me a look like Ha, ha!

The crowds started to leave. But I had to stay. I had to wait so we would find out who was second.

"Go Maddy!" It was Kacey cheering me on. And Isabel! And Claire. They were still there.

Sigh.

So anyway. Orange Team came in second. I ended up fourth.

I felt all bummed! All sad! I almost could have won it!

"Bummer," Kacey said.

"Good try, Maddy," Claire said.

"Well, you still beat my team," Isabel said. She gave me a hug.

"Green Team over here!" Brittany the co-captain yelled. "Maddy, that means you too." Then I heard her say under her breath, "Unfortunately."

chapter 11

We all got in a huddle.

"We're hanging in there," Ryan, our other co-captain said. "The Red Team lost the three-legged race. So we're still in second place behind them. But only by one point! We have one more event to pull ahead!"

"It's the obstacle course!" Brittany interrupted. "Ryan and I are the final hope. We're going to win this thing together! Me and Ryan! Right, Ryan?"

She gave him a smile.

Ooookay. This is SO not going well.

"Uh, right, Brittany," Ryan agreed.

"But even though Maddy just lost us points in the Putt Putt, I'm going to do my best to win it for the team!" Brittany said.

Coach Crosby came over.

"You guys getting psyched up?" He said.

"Yeah!" Everyone yelled. I tried to.

"I was just telling them how it's up to Ryan and me to pull this off," Brittany said. "I'll do a cheer for the Green Team!"

Brittany jumped up.

> "Go Green Team, Go!
> Ryan and Brittany! Will lead us all to victory!
> Brittany and Ryan! I'm not lyin!"

Now I was feeling realllllly nauseous.

"Go, Green Team, UGH!" Brittany yelled.

Go Green Team, ugh!? I looked over at her. She was holding her stomach.

"You OK?" Ryan asked her.

"Yeah," she said. "I was sick this week. I caught germs at Maddy's house. I just need to sit down for a minute."

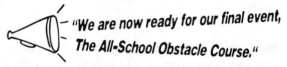

"We are now ready for our final event, The All-School Obstacle Course."

"OK," Brittany said. "That's me! I'm the Green Team. OK! Here I go!" But when she stood up, she was like, "Ohhhh, owwwww, uhhhhhh ..." She sat down and clutched her stomach.

Our co-captain for the Green Team was turning ... GREEN!

Coach Crosby said, "I think I better call her parents." He took out his cell phone and made a call.

"I hope she's OK," Ryan Moore said.

"Me, too," I told him. "I feel really bad. She got sick from my brother!"

Then Coach Crosby went over and started talking to the referee. I could hear a little bit.

"Our co-captain ... sick ... might start vomiting ..."

Coach Crosby came back.

"It appears Brittany's still feeling sick from her stomach flu," Coach said. "Brittany will not be able to participate in the final event."

"A stomach flu?" I asked. "I thought she was sick from my brother's cold."

"No, her mom said it was a stomach bug," Coach said. "Entirely different. Her mother said she caught it from her private cheerleading tutor who had it, too. The doctor said Brittany wasn't contagious anymore. But I guess she's still not feeling well."

A stomach flu? Not a cold? She caught it from her cheer

tutor? HEY!! Brittany kept blaming this thing on me!!!! And Zack!

I felt really mad at Brittany. But then I looked at her.

She looked seriously green.

Looked like she had enough problems!

And then ...

I saw Piper. I saw Piper see Brittany.

Piper went over to her.

"So, YOU'RE here," Piper said to Brittany.

"Yeah," Brittany said. "Brilliant observation."

"Ruin any music contests lately?" Piper asked her.

Brittany didn't answer. She was holding her stomach.

"She's sick, OK?" Petie said to Piper.

"She does look pretty green," Piper said. "Green shirt, green pukey face. I guess you're green with envy? Because our Red Team is crushing your Green Team? Ha! Ha!"

Piper walked away.

Brittany bent over and leaned against the wall. Then I saw Brittany's mother go over to her. They walked away together.

"Green Team, huddle!" Coach Crosby yelled. "We're ready to go into battle! We are in the second place! We can win! Conquer! Defeat! Do you hear me?!!"

YES!!! We all yelled back.

"We have lost our co-captain!" Coach said. "But we have not lost this game! We're bringing in the reinforcements. Our backup player will come through for us!"

"Yes!" We all yelled! "Our backup player will come through!"

"And," Coach said. "Our new backup player will be ...

... MADDY SPARKS!"

chapter 12

OK WHAT??!!!

"HUH!???" Everyone was saying. I knew what they were thinking! Maddy Sparks? Who just totally choked during Putt Putt? She's going to be in the Grand Finale Obstacle Course?!?!?!

And that's what I was thinking too.

"Uh, Coach," I said. "Excuse me, may I speak to you in private?"

We walked over to the side.

"I think there's a mistake," I told him.

"No mistake, Sparks," Coach said. "You're up. When the going gets tough, the tough get going. Be tough."

"Coach," I said. "I'm SO not tough! I mean, hello? I cracked during Putt Putt! You need somebody else!"

"I have confidence in you, Sparks! Besides, there is nobody else," Coach said. "Everyone else already competed in two events. That's the maximum allowed. You're the only one eligible to compete. So ... it's you!"

Ohmigosh. I can't. I can't do that. The grand finale? Obstacle course? In front of everyone? For the championship?

"I think I got Brittany's stomach flu," I said. "I'm going to be sick!!!"

"Sparks," Coach said. "If you don't do this, we are disqualified. The Green Team will be out. Done. Finished. You are our only hope. So get in there and do it for the team"

Oh. My. GOSH!!!!

"The top two teams will face-off in the Grand Finale! All participants, please report to the obstacle course."

That would be me.

Oh! Me and Ryan Moore! I would have to do the obstacle course with Ryan Moore as my partner!

ACKKKKKKKKKKKKKKKKKKKKKKKK!

I repeat.

ACKKKKKKKKKKKKKKKKKKKKKKKKKKK!

"You ready, Maddy?" Ryan asked me.

NO! Not! Never!

"Yerk," I squeaked.

This was SO not going well!!!!

But I had to do it! So we headed over to the start of the obstacle course.

There was a huge crowd! The biggest! Everyone was there to watch us! A bajillion people were waiting to watch me ...

Totally humiliate myself!

 "The Number One Red Team will compete against the Number Two Green Team! The winner will be the winner of the School Spirit Day. The winner will bring home the trophy. Representing the Green Team will be Maddy and Ryan!"

My Green Team went nuts! Yay Green Team! Go Maddy and Ryan!!!

"Representing the Red Team will be Brody and ... Piper!"

Piper?????!!!!

Yes, Piper! Oh NO, Piper!

Oh! That's right! I didn't even think. She's co-captain of the Red Team.

Me vs. Piper.

OHHHHHHHHHHH NOOOOOOOOOOOOO!

Could this get any worse?

The referee told us what we were going to have to do:

- ☆ Run through tires set up on the ground.
- ☆ Climb over a big puffy wall.
- ☆ Squeeze through a tunnel.
- ☆ Solve a puzzle.
- ☆ Ride a zip line to the finish line.

Oh, and under the zip line ... if you fell ... was a mud pit.

ACK! It just did get worse! Mud pit? There's no way I can do this! I would be going into the mud in front of everybody! I just knew it! AUGH!

I was shaky! I was all buzzy! I was wayyyyyy nervous.

"Maddy!" Ryan was waving me over. "Come on!"

We lined up at the starting line. And then Piper whispered to me.

"Hey! It's Clumsy Girl. In the finals! That does it! We just clinched our victory!"

I tried not to listen to her. But I couldn't help it.

"I can't wait to see you trip on the tires! Fall off that wall! Get stuck in the tunnel. Be too dumb to solve a puzzle. And fall in the mud!!!"

Ryan and the Brody guy were lined up first. Then me and Piper would go. Right after them.

The crowd was screaming! The crowd was going crazy!

Piper was giving me dirty looks.

I knew I should ignore her. But that was just way hard! 'Cuz that girl just freaks me out!!!

I was destined for the mud pit! I would win all right. I'd win the Ultimate School Spirit Day **LOSER** Award!!!

And then I heard something ...

"We've got spirit! Yes we do!
We've got spirit! We're the TOO Crew!"

Isabel! Kacey! And Claire! They were cheering for me!

"You can do it, Maddy! Listen to us!!!"

Then I remembered what Isabel had said.

Oh! I got it!

I knew what I had to do. I had to stop looking at Piper! I just had to listen to the TOO Crew! And the Green Team! Yelling! Screaming! Cheering me on!!!

"Guys, on your mark, get set ... GO!"

Ryan and Brody started running! Through the tires! Left, right, left! Right, left, right! Ryan was like through them super fast! They started scrambling up the wall and then ...

ACK! Piper and I were up!

"Girls, on your mark, get set ... GO!"

OK! My turn to go! Now it's my turn! I was running to the tires!

Piper was all left, right, left! I was more ...

Left, right, oops!

Left, oops!

Those things were hard! I was falling way behind. I saw Piper heading to the wall. But I heard the TOO Crew yelling.

"We've got spirit! Yes we do!
We've got spirit! We're the TOO Crew!"

OK, OK, I kept going! Slow! But I didn't give up! And then I was through the tires! OK! To the wall!

I grabbed on to the ledge. It was puffy! It was slippery! I was almost over the wall ...

Oh no! I slipped backwards. Augh! I was going nowhere! I couldn't do it! I couldn't get over the wall!

I was the worst at the obstacle course! I was way BAD.

I was ... like that little wiener dog.

The little wiener dog Zack and I watched on the Pet Channel.

The German Shepherd had zoomed through the course. But the little wiener dog couldn't jump over the wall.

Ryan was the German Shepherd! Piper and that Brody guy? German Shepherds?

But me?

I was like the little wiener dog!!!! Who couldn't jump! Who knocked everything down! Who was pathetic! Just not made for the obstacle course.

I should just give it up NOW!!!

"Maddy's got spirit! Yes it's true!
She's got spirit! She's TOO Crew!"

But I couldn't give up. I mean hey, the wiener dog didn't give up! No! I wouldn't either! (OK! I'm comparing myself to a little wiener dog! But it's true! The little wiener dog kept going!)

And then ... all of a sudden ... I flung myself over the wall! I went over it and ...

Plop! Landed on the soft squishy cushions!

Yeeeees! I DID IT! I made it over the wall!!!!

YEEEESSSS!

But there was no sign of Ryan! Or Piper and Brody! They must be finishing already. Augh!

I ran through the tunnel! Hey, that was easy. And then ran to the giant puzzle. And there was Ryan still at the puzzle.

And Piper and Brody were doing their puzzle, too.

I ran over to Ryan.

"I'm stuck!" Ryan said. "I can't figure this puzzle out!"

I looked over at Piper and Brody. They weren't solving it either!

They were fighting over the puzzle. They wanted to win!

But so did I! I took a deep breath. And I stared at the puzzle. It was a giant puzzle all scrambled up. We had to figure out how to put it together. OK, OK. I moved some pieces around. And then ...

"Wait!" I said. I moved the pieces and ... ohmigosh ...

The pieces fit!

"You did it, Maddy!" Ryan said. "You solved it!"

Then we looked at each other ...

And ran!!! We ran! We left Piper and Brody fighting over the puzzle. Ryan climbed the ladder up, up, up. And then ... he grabbed the handle with both hands. And he zoomed down the zip line.

He zoomed over the mud! And landed! The Green Team was screaming! Yay! Yay! Go! Go!

"OK, Maddy!" he yelled. "You're up!"

Ohmigosh. I had to grab the handle. And then I'd zip down this clothesline looking thing. If I could just hold on, I'd make it to the bottom. If I fell off ...

Mud bath.

I leaned over and grabbed the handle.

And then, right next to me ... Piper was climbing on her side! She was catching up to me! She was grabbing on to the zip line next to me.

"See ya, Snail!" she said! And she zoomed down! Faster than me! I jumped on my zip line and sped down, too ... I was flying!

Ohmigosh! That thing went fast! I zoomed! I was catching up with Piper ... I was catching up and then suddenly ...

Piper gave me a dirty look ... but it didn't last long! Because ...

Piper was looking at ME and not where she was going! And I heard her zip line ...

UNZIP!

Piper's face was like, uh oh! Because she all of a sudden went "Whoa! Whoa!"

She was slipping! I quick-looked to see what happened and I saw Piper ...

Falling ... falling ...

Into the mud pit! PIPER FELL INTO THE MUD PIT!

But I kept zipping.

I held on. I held on tight. And ...

I LANDED AT THE FINISH LINE!

I landed next to Ryan! And everyone went AHHHHHHH!!!

"The Winner of School Spirit Day is ... THE GREEN TEAM!"

We did it! We won! I made it! Everyone was like, MADDY!
MADDY!

Ryan Moore and Derek Hogan lifted me up on their shoulders!
And then everyone was carrying me around yelling ...

GREEN TEAM! GREEN TEAM!

And I could see all the other teams everywhere! And there was
Kacey! Bouncing around all smiley! And Isabel giving me the
thumbs up! And then Claire waving at me!

And then all of a sudden music came over the loudspeaker. It
was a song that always made me feel great. It was ...

My very favorite song by one of my fave groups ... INSPIRE!

Yes, *Things are Looking Up!*

My favorite song was cranking on the loudspeaker! The TOO Crew was with me! I was being carried by my team! A team with Ryan Moore! I was holding a trophy!

How happy was I?

0%————————— 100% !!! 🙂

Coach Crosby called us over to huddle!

"I'm proud of my team today!" Coach said. "You pulled together! You overcame hardship! You met your challenges! You brought the trophy home!"

We were all like **YAY! GREEN TEAM IS NUMBER ONE!**

The school reporter took our team picture. I got to hold the trophy ... with Ryan!!

"Sparks!" Coach Crosby called me over. "You did good. You came through when we needed it. But also, good job on something else. Don't think I didn't notice how you cheered everyone on. You got school spirit, Sparks. You're great at cheering people on ... to victory!"

Wow ... Yay!

That's what I like about cheerleading! That's why I want to be a cheerleader! I like to ... CHEER PEOPLE ON!!!!

I went over to the sponsor area. I had to get my goodie bag, of course! And there was Lauren at the table.

"I saw you do the obstacle course, Maddy!" Lauren said. "You were wonderful!"

"This day has been way wild!" I said. "The TOO Crew was here! I didn't screw up the obstacle course. And when I won, my favorite song by INSPIRE even came on. It was like MAGICAL!!"

Lauren laughed. "Well, I have to confess that I had a hand in the last part. Limited Too was in charge of the music. I saw you win and I couldn't resist. I played your song."

Oh! Well, that explains THAT coincidence!

"But you winning in the first place? That WAS truly magical," Lauren said.

Some girls came to the table.

Lauren handed out goodie bags to them. They were all excited! "Cool! Thanks!" they said.

"I think they were impressed with how well those bags were stuffed," I said.

Lauren laughed.

"Maddy!"

Isabel, Kacey and Claire ran over to me. Lauren gave them their goodie bags.

"Oh, the Green Team gets extra special goodie bags for winning."

She gave me a bag. It had:

- ★ A new CD!
- ★ Lip gloss!
- ★ Candy!
- ★ A Neopet!
- ★ A red and blue slap band!

"Hey, this is cool," I said. "I got a slap band you can record stuff on!"

I pressed a little button and spoke into it, "Hello TOO Crew!" I pressed the play button.

"Hello TOO Crew!" it repeated.

"Hey, cool! Maddy, let me see that!" Isabel asked me. I handed it over.

"So, Maddy," Lauren said. "You deserve a big long break after today. I hope you get some rest."

Uh, yeah ... well actually ... NOT! 'Cuz tomorrow is cheerleading tryouts

Yeek! I'd been so crazy about today that I totally forgot!

"Can't rest," I told Lauren. "I'm trying out for cheerleading tomorrow."

"Well, good luck," Lauren said. "And then get some rest. Because I have big plans for the TOO Crew. It's about time for you all to get another charm for your charm bracelet soon, don't you think?"

Yes! I do!

Isabel gave me back my slap band. "Hey, don't record over this. Just hit the play button tomorrow, OK?"

"Green Team unite! The buses have arrived!" Coach Crosby was yelling.

"I gotta go," I said. We all hugged goodbye. And I went over to my bus. With the rest of the NUMBER ONE GREEN TEAM!

We're #1! #1! #1!

chapter 13

I sat at my kitchen table. I was totally wiped out! Tired! Exhausted! It had been such a huge day! And I couldn't go to bed yet because ...

I hadn't made up my Original Cheer.

"You shouldn't have procrastinated. You shouldn't have waited til the last minute," Mom said.

No offense Mom, but ... no kidding! I mean, I had tried! I had worked on it! I just never got it! I was in a panic!

ACHOO!

A sneeze came from the couch.

"Can you get me some tissues?" Zack called out from the couch.

"Get 'em yourself," I grumbled.

I needed to write my Original Cheer! Something! Anything! I was running out of time. Tryouts were..

TOMORROW! And I had ...

Nothin! Zero! Zippo! Zilch!

> *"My name is Maddy! And I fear!*
> *I will never have an Original Cheer!"*

See what I mean?

"Just one little tissue," Zack whined. Zack moaned. Zack groaned. "I'm soooo sick ..."

"Zack!" I said. "I'm busy."

Zack sat up. Then he flopped down.

"Too weak," he said. "Can't move."

He did look pretty sick. I felt bad for him.

"Oh, all right," I got up. "I'll get your tissues."

"I'm lonely," he said.

"Tell Mom," I said.

"She's on the computer working," Zack whined. "Dad's at the store getting me orange juice."

"Sleep," I said.

"I slept all day," Zack said."Mrs. Huber was here babysitting me. She wanted to teach me to needlepoint. Sleep was the only escape. Please, Maddy! Play with me!"

Oh ... OK. Maybe I was a little too cheerleading, cheerleading, cheerleading! I mean, it's not the most important thing in the world, right?

"Here, maybe I can cheer you up," I said, standing up.

"Get better, Zack!
No more sneezing attack!
Get better soon!
So you can watch a cartoon!"

Zack smiled. "More cheers!" he said weakly. And sneezed again. I handed him a tissue. I took a couple for myself.

"OK, how about this?" I stood in front of him. I bunched up the tissues. I waved tissue pom-poms at Zack.

"Gimme a Z!"

"Z!" Zack said weakly.

"Gimme an A! Gimme a C! Gimme a K!
What does that spell?"

"ZACK!" he yelled. He was getting into it.

"No! It spells annoying little brother!" I yelled. Zack was like "HEY!" But he started laughing.

"Get well soon! Whoo hoo!!" I jumped around! A walkover! A round-off!

Zack clapped. He was seriously smiling. I was smiling, now, too. It felt good to make him smile.

"That was fun when you did my name," Zack said. "And I got to yell, too."

Hm, he just gave me an idea. I went over to the kitchen table and starting writing.

"You're gonna make cheerleading for sure!" Zack said.

"Hey thanks," I told him. "But there are some seriously good people trying out! And they all totally beat me last time."

"What did you screw up last time?" Zack said.

He sounded kinda like Isabel! The TOO Crew had videotaped me.

We found out:

    ★ I hadn't smiled enough!
    ★ I was too klutzy!
    ★ I just wasn't right!

But I'd been practicing.

I'm not the best tumbler. Or the best dancer. Or the best jumper. Was I the best at anything? Was I good enough???

"Do another cheer, Maddy!" Zack said.

I did my Team Cheer for him. He was clapping! And going YEAH!!! He was smiling now. I kicked my best kick! I jumped my best jump! I toe touched my best toe touch! YEAH!

Zack was clapping away for me! I was totally cheering him up!

"That was very good, Maddy!" my mom came into the kitchen. "Very spirited."

Yeah! It felt good! I felt happy I was helping Zack out.

I liked cheering Zack up!

I heard Zack talking to mom.

"Didja see that? I helped Maddy out, Ma." Zack said. "Before I helped her she was all like, blah blah stressed out cheerleading blah. Then I fixed her!"

Well, not exactly. I mean, Zack ... fix me???

But, OK I guess, he kinda did! At least he did give me an idea for my Original Cheer. I'll let him have some credit. Just a little.

I sat down. And started writing!

Just then I received an e-mail from Taylor, my BFF since kindergarten.

```
From: TAYLA
Send To: Maddyblue
Subject: Cheerleading

Good luck w cheerleading tomorrow!!! If I still
lived there I would come cheer u on. but I will
cheer u on from here!!!

LYLAS
xoxox FF, TAYLOR!!!
```

chapter 14

This Journal Belongs to:

Maddy Elizabeth Sparks

Private! Keep Out!!!

Hello from last period choir! The good news is ... I have a sub! That means I don't have to sing in choir today. Which is good. 'Cuz when I sing I sound like wahhhhh!

Way bad.

And I have enough to worry about. Because after choir, I'm not taking the bus home. Because I have ... cheerleading tryouts!

Yes! In less than one hour I will be ... clapping! And

yelling! And cheering! In front of all these people! ACK!!!!

But something weird is happening today and everyone is talking about it.

Brittany is absent, 'cuz she's still sick to her stomach.

I was wondering ...

Would Brittany miss cheerleading tryouts?

Would that mean ... Brittany wouldn't be able to be on the cheerleading team?

I mean, what if Brittany wasn't on the team? What if ... what if I made the team. And Brittany wasn't on it? A whole season without Brittany would be ...

Relaxing! Not stressful! Way much more fun!

But that's mean. Because Brittany luuuvs cheerleading.
So she at least should get to try out. Right?

Yeah, right.

Anyway. She wouldn't miss it.

She's probably home resting up for today. She'll be there.
I'm sure.

Bell rang! G2G to tryouts!!! ACKKKKKKKKKKKK!

OK! So here I am! Walking into the room where I would be waiting
for cheerleading tryouts to start!

I'm way nervous!!! Trying to stay calm! But freaking out!!!

I walked in. Everyone was jumping and twirling and chanting!
Cheering and clapping and bouncing! Practicing! Getting ready!

"Maddy, over here!" Jordan Cooper waved me over. She was standing with our friends Chelsea B and Quinn.

"I'm so nervous!" I told them. "I can't believe it's almost time!"

Then I saw Danielle. With Haley and Brittany. I went over to them.

"Hiiiii Maddy," they said.

"So, Maddy," Brittany said. "Can I talk to you for a sec?"

"Sure ... um, I'm glad you're feeling better," I said.

"I heard you took my spot at the obstacle course," Brittany said.

"Yeah," I said. "I mean, Coach Crosby said I had to –"

"Yeah, right," Brittany said. "I heard you begged Coach to let you do it. So you could be better than me."

WHAT????!! HUH??!!!

"That's so not true!" I said.

"That's what I heard from a reliable source," Brittany said. "So listen. Maybe you pulled off some miracle win yesterday. But not today. I'm sure you wish I was still sick. So you could take my spot on the cheerleading team," Brittany continued. "But sorry to disappoint you –"

"Brittany, I'm your friend," I interrupted her. "Remember coming over to my house? All the fun we had?"

"Whatever," Brittany said. "Look. I'm just saying, stop trying to show off. Stop trying to be better than me. Got it?"

"Brittany, I'm serious," I said. "I'm not trying to show off. I didn't do anything wrong!"

And then I realized something. It was true ...

I had officially HAD ENOUGH OF WORRYING ABOUT BRITTANY!!

"Brittany," I said. "I didn't do anything wrong. Good luck at tryouts."

I started to walk away.

"You're the one that needs the luck, Maddy," Brittany called out. "Maybe you got to steal my spot at the School Spirit Day. Maybe you won the *U-Pick Challenge*. But in cheerleading? I was co-captain AND you didn't make it. And it's gonna happen again. Today!"

I kept walking.

chapter 15

Haley and Danielle were looking at me like ... WHAT just happened?

I didn't have time to think! Because then ... a door opened and ...

"GIRLS! It's time to get started!" said one of the gym teachers.

OK. This is the deal:

    ★ Everyone will get a sheet of paper with a number.
    ★ Then we would try out one by one in the gymnasium.
    ★ First we will do the Team Cheer.
    ★ Then, we will perform our Original Cheer.

The gym teacher told us all the rules. What to do. What not to do.

Ohmigosh! I was so nervous!!!!!!!!!

OK! I was number 19. So, I would have to wait awhile. I put my number in my backpack. We were supposed to just wait. Sit there. Not make any noise. The gym teacher said we could do our homework or something.

Yeah, right! Like I could do my homework right now?

NOT!

I just sat there. Being way nervous!

Danielle was up first.

"Go, Danielle!" I said. "You can do it!!!!"

We all sat there. Trying to hear what was going on!

"Can you hear anything?" Jordan whispered to me.

I listened. Nothing ... nothing. Then we heard some clapping. Applause!

That must mean Danielle was finished!

The gym teacher came in and called Number 2. Number 2 was Brittany.

Brittany stood up. She walked past me toward the door of the gym. Then she stopped for a minute. She leaned against the door.

Then she went into the gym.

I wasn't sure. But I didn't think she looked too good. Brittany went into the gym.

We waited to hear the applause to show she was done. But then all of a sudden we heard this ...

Ohhhhhhhhhhhhhhhhhh!

And the door busted open.

Brittany came in! She shlumped down on the ground. Haley ran over to her.

"Too nauseous," Brittany said. "Can't jump. Can't flip. No double back handspring."

Brittany's mom came in. She's the coach of the cheerleaders! She was talking to Brittany.

Everyone was like, "What's going on! Brittany is too sick to try out! Will Brittany have to drop out of cheerleading tryouts! What will happen?!"

"Girls," Brittany's mom said. "I have an announcement. We have a change in plans. The co-captains of the football cheerleading squad will not have to try out. They will automatically make the new squad."

The co-captains had been Amanda ... and Brittany!

"Figures," Jordan whispered.

"Instead they will be judges," her mom announced.

Amanda was like, "Oh! Really? Wow! Cool!"

But the rest of us were like, "Really? Huh?"

Judges? Amanda and Brittany would be judges?!!!

Brittany stood up. She smiled. She and Amanda went into the gym with Brittany's mom.

"Yeesh. That Brittany knows how to work it," Jordan whispered to me. "She's too sick to try out! So she turns into a judge!"

Huh.

Moving on! Number 3 was up!

Chelsea B's turn. She looked all stressed. She wasn't even smiling.

"Go Chelsea!" I whispered. "Don't forget to smile!"

Then everyone went! Haley! Shana! Quinn! Lots more people! Then Jordan!

"Good luck!" I said to her. "Wait! Your ponytail!"

Her bow was all crooked.

I helped Jordan fix the bow on her ponytail.

"Thanks, Maddy!" Jordan said. And went in.

We waited. We heard the applause.

And then ... after Jordan ... they called number 19. That was ...

ME!!!!!!

OK. OK. OK! My turn! I was up! I jumped up!

"Bring your permission slip," the gym teacher reminded me.

Oh yeah! My permission slip! I reached into my backpack to
look for my form. Looking through all my stuff ... I pushed past
my notebook ... my slap band. Oh yeah! My slap band. Isabel had
told me to play it today. So I pressed the play button on it ...

> *"You've got spirit, yes you do!*
> *You'll rock your tryouts! Says the TOO Crew!!!!"*

A message from Kacey and Isabel and Claire!!!!!!!!!!! They had
recorded it on my slap band!

How cool was that!!!!

I thought about everything they told me. I had to smile. To look
right at the judges! To jump high! To stay cool! To be SPIRITY!!!

I felt READY!

I found my permission slip.

OK. I WAS READY.

I followed the gym teacher into the gym.

OH! MY!! GOSH!!!

The gym was crowded! There were so many people in the bleachers. People from my school! And parents! I saw my Mom and Dad up there. They were looking at me like, Go Maddy!

ACKKKKKKKKKKKKKKK! My head was all fuzzy. My legs were all shaky. I turned to the judge's table. There were two gym teachers, another teacher, Brittany's mom, Amanda and Brittany.

So weird to see Brittany at the judge's table.

All right. First, my Team Cheer!

Ready? OK!

I did my Team Cheer! I jumped! I clapped. I remembered to smile! I stuck my landings! I nailed it. YEAH!

I looked at the judges.

Brittany's mom was kinda smiling at me. The two gym teachers were kinda smiling at me. Some woman I didn't know was kinda smiling at me. Amanda was kinda smiling at me.

Brittany was ...

Not smiling at me. SO not smiling at me. Looking at me like ...

Rolling her eyes. Like Maddy? Making cheerleading? I don't even think so.

I started feeling ...

Stupid. Uncomfortable. Weirded-out.

And then I remembered what Isabel had said ...

"What if someone gives you a dirty look? Like a judge or something? You need to be prepared."

And she was right! It did happen! Brittany was giving me dirty looks! I remembered what I was supposed to do if that happened:

    ☆ Ignore the mean looks!
    ☆ Smile!
    ☆ And ... think of people who make me happy!

Like ...

My other friends! The TOO Crew! And my family!

I turned to look at the bleachers. Mom and Dad were all giving me the thumbs up. Zack was waving.

And then ... I saw them ... THE TOO CREW WAS THERE!

KACEY! AND ISABEL! AND CLAIRE!!!!!

No seriously! They were really there! In my school bleachers!

Cheering me on!!!!!!!!!

"We're ready for your Original Cheer, Maddy," Brittany's mother said.

OK. Here goes ...

> *"I've got spirit! YEAH! Tons of spirit! YEAH!*
> *I've got spirit ... lots of spirit..*
> *And now ... I want to hear it ... from you!"*

I turned to the bleachers. And I pointed to the left bleachers. And yelled:

> *"Do YOU have spirit? Say YEAH!"*

Everyone in the bleachers kinda looked at each other. Like, is she talking to us? So I yelled again.

"Do YOU have spirit? Say YEAH!"

And the TOO Crew yelled back ...

"YEAH!"

Then the crowd got it! And when I yelled it again, everyone yelled back ...

"YEAH!!!"

And I yelled out ...

"If you've got spirit, clap your hands!"

So everyone in the bleachers clapped!

And I yelled out ...

"If you've got spirit, stomp your feet!"

STOMP! STOMP!! STOMP!!!

The bleachers were shaking!!!

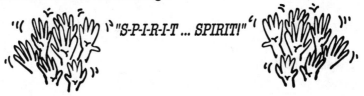

"S-P-I-R-I-T ... SPIRIT!"

I did a cartwheel! I did a round-off! I waved to the crowd! I waved to the judges!

The crowd was clapping and yelling and screaming and going WOO HOOO!

And they were all smiling! And screaming! And I saw my parents yelling! And clapping!

And Zack was waving ... pom-poms made of tissues!!!!

And Kacey and Isabel and Claire were all jumping and waving and cheering!!

YEAH! YEAH! YEAH!

And at the judge's table ...

The judges were smiling! Even Brittany's mother was smiling! And Brittany?

I don't know!

And I didn't even bother to look at her!

I was smiling! And then I was waving! And then I was finished!

IT WAS OVER!!!!!!!!

I ran off the gym floor! I ran out to the hallway. All the other girls were out there waiting.

"What were you doing in there?!" Haley ran over and demanded.

"We heard all this cheering! And clapping! And stomping!" Danielle said. "Way noisy! Way crazy!"

"Did you get them all cheering like that?" Jordan asked me. "Wow-ness! You must have been super spirity!"

Yes!

I was!

chapter 16

When everyone had tried out, we all went back into the gym. My Mom, Dad and Zack came over.

"Congratulations, honey," Mom said. "That was wonderful."

"Yeah, that was awesome," Zack said. "Everyone was like all noisy! All crazy and stuff!"

"Good job," my Dad said.

"The best part though was when that Brittany went out there," Zack said. "And she was like, all floppy. All sickish. She looked like she was going to puke her guts up! Heh, heh, that was awesome."

Zack made puking noises.

"Zack," my mom warned. "Be nice. The poor girl was sick."

"That's no poor girl. That's Brittany. She's always mean to me," Zack said. "She makes ME want to puke."

Hm.

Then Kacey and Isabel and Claire came running up to me!

"You were so smiley!" Kacey said.

"You were so jumpy!" Claire said.

"You were so spirity!" Isabel said.

"Thanks!" I said.

"Sorry we were late," Claire said. "Bruno had to pick everyone up after school and drive here."

"I just can't believe you guys are here!" I said.

That was so cool the TOO Crew was there.

Suddenly ...

There was an announcement.

"Would all cheerleading tryout participants please report to Room 3A. We will announce the results."

"You find out the results NOW?" Kacey asked. "Wow! We had to wait til the next day for our results to be posted!"

"We had to wait THREE days," Isabel said.

"You better get in there, Maddy," Claire said.

I waved bye! And I went into Room 3A. Everyone was all nervous. Everyone was all shaky. I sat down between Danielle and Jordan.

Brittany's mom walked in.

"You girls did such a wonderful job," she said. "I was very impressed. Unfortunately we can't have everyone. I will now hand you a piece of paper with your evaluation. It will tell you if you have made the team."

Ohmigoshohmigoshohmigosh.

This was it.

"Feel free to go somewhere private to read it," Brittany's mother said.

Brittany's mother went around the room. She handed out papers.

Everyone was like ... EEEK!!!

And I was like ... YIKES!!!!!!!!

I took the paper that said #19. I went out to the hallway and walked down a little ways.

I needed to be alone. To find out. Would it be ...

YES.

Or.

NO.

I unfolded my paper.

Jumps ... pretty good.

Motions ... pretty good.

Tumbling ... good.

Spirit ... WOW! I scored really high at spirit!

I kept reading ... reading ... and then I saw it.

**WELCOME Maddy Sparks
to the Basketball Cheerleading Squad
CONGRATULATIONS!!!!!!!!**

Oh. My. Gosh.

I MADE CHEERLEADING!!!! AHHHHHHHHHHHHHHHHHH!!!

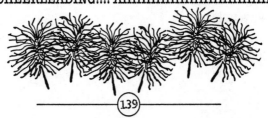

I ran down the hallway and looked around! Who could I tell! My friends? My Mom? My Dad? And then I saw ...

Kacey! And Isabel! And Claire!

They were standing there looking at me like ...

WELL?

And I went ...

AHHHHHHHHHHHHHHHHHHHHHHHHHHHHHHHHHHHH!!!!!!!

"You did it!" Claire screamed.

"Yay Maddy!" Kacey yelled.

"Go, girl!" Isabel said.

I thought about the day I had met the TOO Crew. I'd been so bummed! It had been a baaaaad day! Because I hadn't made cheerleading and all my friends had!!!

But now ...

Even though I didn't make it the first time, I'd tried again.
I didn't give up!

I practiced really hard!

I gave it my best!

And I made the team!!!

And the TOO Crew had helped me!!!!!!!

I looked at Kacey and Isabel and Claire. And I started saying ...

"We got spirit, yes we do!"

And they finished it with me ...

"We've got spirit! We're the TOO Crew!!!!!!!!!"

Happy Face Rating:

 out of

the end ... for now that is!

Because it's not really the end! Not even close! And wait til
you see what happens next! Stay tuned!

OK, bye! 'Cuz I have to go celebrate now that I am a cheerleader!!! Yup, after all my hard work ... I made it!!

But don't worry! I'll be back really soon in Episode #6!

OK, here's a sneak preview of what's going to happen next. There's this dog shelter that is opening by me! And guess what?!! They need people to volunteer. YES! It's true! I'm going to help with cute little doggies!!!

So get Tuned In! And check out Episode #6! Coming soon exclusively at Limited TOO!!!

♡

CU Soon! Luv ya!!!! ♡

Maddy